Acknowledgements

Special thanks to my supportive partner Rachael and my Mother Beryl who is always there for me and to my Sister Jan Webber Author of the Betty Illustrated Children's books.

Also by David Dowson

Chess for Beginners
Chess for beginners Edition 2
In to the Realm of chess Calculation
Nursery Rhymes
The Path of a Chess Amateur by David Dowson
CHESS: the BEGINNERS GUIDE eBook:
DOWSON, David:

Table of Contents

CHAPTER ONE: ATTEMPT

January 15, 1986, 18:36 hours

Home time. I leave the Bureau and head off home in my car, It's a dark wet night and I'm traveling behind a white transit van with blacked out windows, I decide to overtake the van but the van increased in speed not allowing me to overtake, I slowed down to return to my position behind the van, the van then also slows down preventing me to return behind it, so I decide to change gear quickly to increase my speed suddenly, to get around the van but to my surprise the van then unexpectedly lurched forward increasing its speed again stopping me from overtaking it, by then a car appeared in the opposite direction its headlights blinding me. I couldn't avoid the car as the van prevented me from getting back in my lane, I tried to go faster to get a quick look at the drive of the van, but it was to no avail as he picked up his speed as well, I was trying to find a way back that I didn't notice just how close the incoming vehicle was. We had a head on collision which all happened in slow motion. The collision wasn't as fatal as both I and the incoming driver tried to drop speed at the very end. The vehicles however were damaged significantly. I rushed down trying to see to the welfare of the driver and to see if I could catch a glimpse of the van driver who stopped as if to see if I was dead but before I could get very close to him, he drove away.

The accident was huge, wasn't fatal as we both walked out of our respective vehicles alive, but it didn't leave me without any scar. I experienced after the accident an uncontrollable, involuntary twitch.

A nodding of my head, and uncontrollable utterance of words, it was then that my life would change forever. I saw numerous doctors, physiotherapists, neuroscientists and even psychiatrists trying to find the solution to my nervous disorder if that is what it was anyways because that was the opinion each one of them had.

The white van, I tried my hardest to look at its number before it drove away, it was 496 and I could swear I had seen that van before, but I wasn't sure from where and thoughts flooded my mind. Who wanted me dead? Of course, I had been an agent for over 10 years, I might have upset some of the top brass but not for the wrong reasons, I put them out of commission but only because it was the right thing to do. The van looked to me like a GCHQ MOPD reconnaissance vehicle (a vehicle used by the agency for information gathering) but why would the agency want me out of the picture? I became weary of everything, of everyone but I checked myself knowing that paranoia wasn't the solution. I needed to get back to work, I needed to run a trace on the white van before drawing a conclusion.

I resumed work at the bureau as usual after a short time off trying to sort out some basic issues regarding the accident and the twitching but work as I knew it was gone. My security clearance had been revoked; I couldn't access the basic records. I couldn't track the van's record from any computer at the bureau with my login information. It seemed like I had been blocked or something. I tried to access the physical files at the records room, but I was refused access into the room. "Order from the superiors" as I was told. It was at that point that thing started to smell fish. Somebody wanted to get rid of me. Had they realized I was the invincible man? Everyone became suspicious to me. My life as I knew it was coming down right in front of me. It was bound to happen sooner or later as it had happened with some of the best agents out there but not while I still feel I was still of use to my country.

CHAPTER TWO: IT BEGINS

A lot of unanswered questions are already up in the air. My name is David Scarlett, I am an intelligence for the British secret service, the GCHQ. I served 20 years in allegiance to my country. Underground without the knowledge of my wife. I have been married to Carla for over two decades and everything seemed well at the time. It looked like love, but I could hardly say it was, I was always away and always had excuses as to why I was away. I did a pretty good job. The secret service did teach us extensively how to convince our spouses about what we do.

Up until 1999, it was good until I was attacked. That incidence changed my life. I have been a mess and I have been unable to keep my marriage together. I wouldn't blame Carla though. She had been with me through my good and my bad, through thick and thin. In sickness and in health and all those other shits they say at the altar. She had her demons, but I wasn't there to help her fight them.

I felt like I had a reason to end my life, I have felt that way since the incident in 1999. I didn't do anything to earn me the title, Target. I focused on my problems and in my very before, my wife slipped into a depression. The realization of her problems brought me back to reality and made me realise I should stick around for her. Carla's attempted suicide left me shaken. It would be nice to say that our marriage has been rock solid since then but that is far from the case. It seems like love had walked out the door as we both were trying hard to sort out our respective problems.

November 1, 2006

Things were not going well between me and Carla, the arguments keep coming, we fight about one thing or the other every day and end up going to sleep with our backs turned against each other. This was just like every other day, we had argued about something, I can't even place my mind on exactly what it was as the arguments would come every day. It was like every other day, we had both gone to bed angry. I laid back on my bed blaming myself for the failure in my marriage. I had to put in more effort to fix it, but Carla wasn't giving me much of the support I need. It was exhausting but I couldn't give up. I wanted to fix my marriage but what about myself. The accident in 1999 had left me even more broken than Carla. The only reason why I hadn't killed myself was Carla and now she was adding up to the pressure. I had to maintain a cool head for myself and my wife.

November 2, 2006

The argument from the night before was heated and we both woke up tensed and angry. We were in the same house, we didn't have breakfast together and it was afternoon and we still had not talked properly to each other just the occasional hi, ok, if I must. I went out today to the restaurant by myself. Normally, we'd go out together, but the argument was heated that I went out alone and had a burger and chips, I was feeling down, and I started to hallucinate again. It was happening again like it usually did every now and then. I saw a man, I feel like I see him on the outside but clearly, he is in my head, he had a knife in is hand and he urged me to kill, kill, kill. It's driving me crazy, people across the way enjoying their meal, oblivious to the fact that I was having a mental breakdown. I managed to pull myself together and hurl my broken self-home, but it felt like a wrong decision as always. Carla tried to use alcohol to fight her depression.

The argument with Carla never ends. When I think that I have finished one, another begins. Whenever I get drunk, I get abusive,

CHAPTER THREE: AN AGENTS TALE

December 25, 2006

Christmas day, I'm at my family's house in Salisbury Wiltshire, I feel at home in Salisbury. Out there, I meet so many of my friends with whom I worked in the service as well as my friends from childhood. It takes my mind away from the troubles at home. My brothers and friends all gathered in one place drinking, eating and having fun. Of course, the question on everybody's lips was "where is Carla?" it came from every angle, but I had to explain to them in such a way that they'd understand all is not well but not enough to give them a clear picture of the problems in my marriage.

I had friends who had served in the agency with me, with whom we could discuss all about our past in the service and reminisce for old time's sake while at Salisbury. I had left Carla at her parent's, I needed some sort of rebuild during my brothers, both by birth and war.

Time to seek help and support from my brothers, I have been hoodwinked, put to death and resurrected, I have found peace and fulfilment, in search of light and the word, both I have found. Vailed in ritual and allegory, for I am a Sovereign Prince Rose Croix of Herodom, fidelity, fidelity, fidelity may God preserve the Craft. We have a good time reminiscing of the years of service, of childhood and each person talking about their marriages. I sit still with no words to join in the festivities, I remember the rigors of some missions and the past in General. As I take a sip of my glass of brandy, I fall into the warm embrace of my memory as it took me back to the beginning. Where it all started. Forty years ago, the year I joined the service.

September 1, 1976

Salisbury Cathedral Wiltshire England

I was a young impressionable 21-year-old Cambridge university graduate, eager, seeing the world in a whole new light. It was new to me, not Salisbury but life as a Cambridge university graduate. I could do whatever I want now, I could be my own man and make my own decisions without being told what to do. I stood in awe of the magnificent religious structure gazing at the stained-glass windows squinting as I looked and stared at the stained-glass windows of the cathedral. The sun rays reflecting off the glass windows made it difficult to see but it was not to stop me as I placed my hands just over my eyes lids so I could behold the beauty that was the cathedral. It was then that I noticed a sign that I would come across some years later, "David, David" a voice brought me back from my gaze as I scrambled to see who was calling out my name.

"The bishop is waiting come quickly" he said, "quickly your late" he said as he gestured pointing the direction, we scampered through the cathedral and as we did so, I noticed a Calmness, a stillness that I have never felt before. "This way, go through the door he's waiting for you over there" he said. As I walked through the door, it was a visit to the bishop, but I didn't know that that visit would change my life forever.

A voice from inside, calm and firm, gentle but assertive said "come in and close the door", I walked gently into the large imposing office. I looked around to get a glimpse of where I was. Of course, I was in the cathedral, but it seemed like this study commanded more holiness than the other parts of the cathedral. It was broad, wall to wall covered with all manners of books, I was sure I saw almost every version of the bible and different other religious books. I walked forward towards a large desk covered in papers, a man dressed in religious robes was sat at the desk "hello David, I'm bishop john Clever, please sit down and tell me all about yourself".

I shyly started, slowly talking all about myself curious as to what was to follow. I came to the end of my short history of life, then he hit me with a question, "who are God's chosen children" he asked. I was stumped as I did not take much notice in religion lessons. I didn't know what to respond. I didn't want to say the wrong things to the bishop. He seemed a man well respected, and I wouldn't want to be the one who answers foolishly as well. Then I guessed "the Israelites" I said. He didn't make a sound or show any emotion, but he did make a note.

I continued my religious studies attending every day for six months. Listening to what the bishop was saying, and I started to get into it, delving deeper into the religious nuances. At the end of my studies, he presented me with an ornate church of England headed signed letter to profess that I have undergone religious studies in the Christian faith and confirmed that I was a believer in Christianity in accordance with the church of England, signed by the arch bishop of

Canterbury. This I had to present to the Saudi Officials with my passport before they would issue me a with visa to enter the kingdom of Saudi Arabia, I do not know of any other person that had to undergo this process to get a visa, things were so different then.

I arrived at 1 am Saudi time the door of the plane opened and then it hit me, the heat wave came at me guns blazing like a rushing win only without the pleasure that a wind brings. It was clearly different from England. The sun hung around like it was waiting for tips for doing a perfect job. You wouldn't be able to survive the heat without support from water or juice or something of the sort. I paid attention to the weather not realizing the culture shock that was just around the corner.

As we dropped, the sounds of Islamic prayers from nearby mosques filled the air. It was weather, culture and religion like I had never seen before. One particular sound repeated itself more than others and I was able to pick up on that even though I didn't know the meaning. Allahu Akbar, was heard everywhere while I came down from the plane. Over the next six years of my life, I'd hear that Islamic phrase more times than I'd eat food. It was sacred, that I was sure of as I walked.

I noticed a man, dressed in a mustard suit who had long hair packed into a ponytail. He looked at me and used his index finger to cross over his upper and lower lips as if to tell me to shut up, he communicated glancing at me. I was surprised as I didn't know the man and clearly didn't understand why he was shutting me up. Little did I know I would meet him again in circumstances that I could never have thought about now, but one thing would be made clear however, his presence proved really important not just me but for the entirety of England, offering me a life changing experience? He was closely followed by another man, about six feet five. I sat by him on the plane and the only conversation I had with him during the ten hours flight was when he said to me quite openly and not discreetly "I suppose you're a terrorist" well I was shocked not just at the question but the manner in which it was asked. I was carrying a white hand luggage with big red letters on it saying Great Britain. Containing all my information and documents. I politely told him I was the deputy finance attaché to Saudi Arabia.

I descended the steps of the plane unaware that I would see both of the men sometime later, at the British embassy, were I was acting as the deputy finance attaché. I had been recruited from Cambridge University, it was a strait forward suggestion "would you like to enter the intelligence service" a man asked in a forward manor not caring who was around or listening. I at once said yes, it was a chance to fulfil a childhood dream. It was a privilege to serve my country as an intelligence agent but what pushed me the most to accept the offer was the perceived thrill, I would get from being a spy of some sort. When the question was asked, the first thought that came to mind were of James Bond. I would be like 007 going around the world saving people. I didn't think much of what the job was at the time.

1:10 am Saudi Local time

As I reached the bottom of the aircraft stairs, there was a black Cadillac which very well seemed like it was waiting for me, a man smartly dressed stood at the rear of the opened door. Mr Scarlet, he said like he had received a briefing about me. I paused, then said "yes", "I am here to take you to your hotel", he said, in perfect English.

Cautious about safety, I tried to scan my environment carefully to see if nothing was off before entering the car of a man I had never met in my life. I looked around the area and noticed that the other two passengers of the flight who were left were no longer there. That was nothing to cause a worry, so I walked closer to the car gently and carefully. The man could visibly see concern laced over my entire actions, but he was calm, however. His personality to me was as perfect as his spoken English.

I slowly got into the car and the driver shut the door and he proceeded to the Continental hotel. Clutching my attach case, knowing that I had a 9mm Barretta pistol and two fully loaded magazines, a gun of my own preference. This was the benefit of being an embassy official, no personal checks. The trip to the hotel from the airport was quick. No words were said between us. He kept his cool not allowing even a sound leave his lips. I thought to myself that he must be a professional of some sort. The normal cab drivers in England would have said so much that you could write a book from the stories. I didn't say a word either. My silence was drawn more as a result of caution than anything. I heard a lot of stories about the Arab world before coming here and I needed to put myself in a situation where my safety was always in my own hand.

01.30 am Saudi local time

I arrive at the hotel it was very cosmopolitan. The driver goes out and opened the car door for me to come down, I was feeling a little important with all the things he was doing for me. He said that he would be on his way now but that he would be ready to pick me up at 08.30 am local time. I just gave a slight nod as he opened the boot and got my luggage out. I still had my case in my hand, I held it firmly like a child who didn't want to go missing holding her mom.

I got to my room, I sat on the edge of the bed quietly deep in my own thoughts of the operation ahead and a mixture of personal thoughts that I tried to block out, there was no place for personal thoughts whilst in the service especially now, the city parts was loud, you could hear the horns of cars and the engine sounds as they drove by, the sounds of prayers from a nearby mosque filled the air. I couldn't make sense of what they were saying but their attention to religion struck me as remarkable. As my subconscious tried to settle in with the city, it almost pushed away the thoughts of my mission but maintaining focus was so important to an agent as it held your very life in its grasps. The moment you allow yourself lose concentration, that moment, you have placed your life and that of your associates in the hands of the enemy whoever they were. When this crossed my mind, I returned my thoughts to carrying out my mission. I laid down on the bed thereafter toggling between the surroundings of Saudi Arabia and my mission.

As the warm embrace of the night came close to me, I started to ponder about the next order of business. My stay at the embassy, what would it feel like? This was new to me, but I was sure it was going to be ok. The rest of my life would take a course, the course that the success of my mission here in Saudi Arabia followed. This was the defining moments of my life and I had to make sure I got it right. These were the thoughts in my mind as I slowly faded out into dream land. It never gets old, the beauty of a good night's rest, those were the final words my mind whistled in my ear as I slept off.

CHAPTER FOUR: THE JOURNEY

January 3, 1977

08:00 am Saudi Arabia time

This was it, the beginning of my life as a member of the intelligence agency. I had mixed feelings. On one side, I was overly excited for what was to come and on the other side, I was uncertain about what was to come. What if I fail? What if most importantly, I die? I was worried but I tried to shrug it off quickly, no need to be negative, a little optimism can't kill, I said to myself as I headed for the room window, to open the blinders. I looked through the window and for the time of the year that it was, there wasn't that many festivities going on. It was January 3rd, I expected it to be like In England with the candy canes and the dress up Santa and the rein deer but that wasn't it, this was Saudi Arabia. There was no Christmas, there was no new year, it was your regular every day. It was weird to me but being a really open-minded person, I accepted the religion and tradition that I met there.

I tried to while away time as I wait for the chauffeur to come pick me up for my first day at the embassy. I washed myself, applied lotion as I prepared for the day. I called for room service, and I was given an egg omelette. I ate it in a hurry not wanting to waste a second of anybody's time when he finally got here. He was like a programmed machine, at exactly 8:30, he was already at my room door knocking gently, waiting for me to follow him and I duly obliged picking what was left of my stuff and followed him like a schoolchild, following his teacher.

The trip this time wasn't as quiet as the first one, as we boarded the Cadillac vehicle and was about to leave, I asked him gently "what is your name mate?" the chauffeur turned and replied to Anwar, and I smiled. I wasn't in the mood for much of a chit chat, but I felt this was it, I was going to be seeing more of Anwar on a daily basis, and I might as well get acquainted with the lad. "I don't know how you do it over here but where I'm from, if you pick a lad from the airport, you give him some information about the city" Anwar clearly was educated but wasn't much of a talker, he turned back to me for a split second and said, "I'm just doing what I was told to do". Clearly, I wasn't going to get much of a conversation from Anwar, so I just relaxed myself and waited for him to drop me at the embassy.

We got to the embassy, this was it, my new posting, and I was going to nail this and do myself a lot of good and serve my country better. Anwar stopped the car, turn off the engine, came down and rushed to my door and opened it for me. I came down, I gestured a handshake for Anwar and this time, he obliged me, and he shook my hand and bowed in respect for me. He was clearly older, but he was so well mannered. I walked into the embassy, greeted at the gates by members of the British military, soldiers armed and ready to dispel any threat whatsoever. I got in and I met with Col Harry Crawford, the defence attaché himself who seemed like he had been waiting a while for the aid or like something was up that he couldn't handle alone, that he needed to tell someone about. I looked round like a child who just moved into a new apartment. What was striking the most was that I hadn't received a mission briefing or why my very first posting was to the Middle Eastern nation of Saudi Arabia, but I was certain I would find out soon.

Col Harry took me around, introducing me to all the staffs that I needed to know, he briefed me of everything I needed to know. Before he showed me to my office, he told me that there was someone I needed to know. I wondered who it was. I followed the Col to an upstairs office, it had a thoroughly designed wooden door, it looked like whoever was inside was a very important member of staff, maybe the High commissioner or something.

I adjusted myself ensuring I looked very smart. I was eager to impress on the first day and maybe continue impressing throughout my stay in Saudi Arabia before my next posting would come. The Colonel knocked gently on the wooden door and a croaked voice from inside the office shouted, "come in, will yah?" I was a little bit amused by the response, but I tried to keep myself in check. I followed the Colonel inside where we met two men seated on two chairs, one in front of a desk, probably the owner of the office, he was wearing an expensive suit, I could tell just by looking at it. It was a Desmond Merrion suit, a very expensive brand in the UK, I didn't know that I would only realize when he said so himself. The other man on the opposite side of the table, dressed a lot simple, a shirt tucked in and a tie and a simple pair of trousers and a neatly polished shoe.

Both men seemed to have been deeply engaged in a conversation before we walked in, the colonel saluted the man in the suit and said to me, "I believe you know who he is?", I responded quickly "yes sir, I do sir" I didn't before we entered the office but thanks to the name tag on the door, I could identify that he was the high commissioner His excellency James Perkins. I was so excited; I could literally crap myself. I was standing before the British High Commissioner to Saudi Arabia. He stretched out as his hands to request a handshake, I hurriedly reciprocated the action and shook hands with him while bowing my head in respect and honour. He does deserve it, to have climbed this high in his career whereas I was just starting mine was something to be respected for.

The other man looked less flashy but commanded his respect in his own way, the Colonel pointing to the man, found him as Mr Ronald Bishop, he was the finance attaché at the embassy. It made sense now, he is the one I was to work with. I knew I had to make an excellent first impression, so I greeted him, and he stretched out his hand as if to gesture a handshake which I obliged. The High commissioner looked at me and spoke "welcome to Riyadh Mr?" "David sir, David Scarlett", I replied with stuttering words. He smiled and pointed at Mr Ronald "I believe you know you are working with him? Do your best son. He'll bring you up to speed. Welcome again to the kingdom of Saudi Arabia".

CHAPTER FIVE: MISSION BRIEFING

The next few days of working at the embassy in Saudi Arabia went fine but David could not understand why he was there at Saudi Arabia. He wasn't a diplomat if anything, he was an agent. He wanted action, anyhow they come but Mr Ronald and Col Harry and even the High commissioner didn't seem like they had much in store for him. He waited patiently although he was starting to become impatient. I'd go to work every other day and pay attention to finance. Of course, as a finance graduate, I was doing what I loved but as an agent, I was getting close to zero satisfaction.

It was frustrating but I knew it would happen sooner than later. I was sitting on my office chair punching the numbers when Ronald or Ronnie like he liked to be called sent for me. It was the moment of truth. Ronnie himself was an undercover agent, oblivious to everyone who worked at the embassy except maybe the high commissioner. I walked into his office, and he said in a silent but firm tone. "This is it son, the moment I know you've been waiting for". He handed me a file which I collected unsure of what was going on. I opened the file and brought out papers having financial transactions.

"This is why you were sent here son", his words break the focus I had on the paper as I looked up to meet his gaze which was fixated on me. At that exact moment, Col Harry and the commissioner walked in. Ronnie continued speaking "those are financial records that the GCHQ had been tracking for a while now, they belong to a Saudi Arabian by name Mustapha Al-Aziz. You'd wonder why his financial transactions concerns the United Kingdom, right. Easy question, he has holdings in major companies in the UK and recently, one of the firms he owns was tracked sending a huge amount of money into the accounts of Megatrax, a company that is suspected of producing weapons. When confronted by British authorities, they claimed to just be procuring raw materials. Al-Aziz has been tied to various extremist movements but for want of evidence, has walked free. We need you to put an eye on his financial movements and involvements. The second you see anything suspicious; you report to any one of us".

Suddenly, Saudi Arabia was looking exactly like I thought it would be, I went into my fantasy world for some seconds as Ronnie spoke. I saw myself dressed in suits, pointing a gun at some random Arabian guy, clearly my mind was creating a persona of Al-Aziz, but I wasn't even sure if the face of the person I saw was real. I was brought back to reality when Ronnie asked if I had any question concerning the briefing I just received. They all could tell that I was bursting with excitement from being handed my first intelligence mission. "Get this right and it clearly won't be your last" Ronnie said to me as they all headed for the door. "Oh, and just so you know kid, this is top secret, no unauthorised personnel find out and definitely nobody hears about it". I nodded in response as they headed out of the briefing room.

I picked up the files, I walked into my office in stealth mode like a ninja avoiding prying eyes until it was the right time to strike, I locked the door, sat down on the chair, brought out the files and looked at each sheet with rapt attention like I was going to see a line that pointed me in the right direction. I was so eager to impress that it was so difficult to notice anything that happened around me that wasn't happening on the paper. I wasn't going to let anybody down. This was the beginning of a new super-agent and that was me.

The day flew by, and nothing came up, day became days and day's weeks but still nothing extremely suspicious was happening that seemed to attract my attention. I was almost frustrated and paying less attention to the online activity of all the bank accounts that the British intelligence had brought up relating to Mustapha Al-Aziz. I thought this was it, my first mission was over before I knew it, after abandoning the documents for over a week, I pick them up and notice that amidst a lot of new entries into the accounts of Megatrax, and a lot were coming from unknown accounts. It was strange, how would a multi-billion-pound company be dealing with unknown transactions and most importantly, if they took part in selling arms to a suspected English Arabian billionaire extremist, why couldn't they hide their tracks a little bit? It smelt fishy but the instruction was to report at once if anything didn't seem right.

I rushed out of my office, knocked at Ronnie's office where I met him and Harry talking about something, that wasn't my concern. I had made a breakthrough. One I questioned but I knew I had to say something sooner or later. They ushered me a seat, but I was too eager to sit down. "Breathe son and then tell us what you have to tell us". I tried to catch my breath, but it wasn't that I was short of breath, it was that I was too excited about finding out something that might be helpful. "It isn't conclusive yet sir but there has been a trend on the accounts of all parties that you sent to me. They were all quiet recording what seemed their normal daily expenses but recently, there has been activity, a significant number of them. There has been a lot of transactions entering into megatrax from unknown sources, individually not enough to cause a stir but together, just around the amount where we have to be worried. The part that seems unclear to me is why such a corporation would want to tarnish its image. I get money is involved but shouldn't they be more focused on hiding their tracks by receiving such money elsewhere. I know tracking money like we are doing now is new tech and not a lot of people can do it, but its bollocks to have your affairs out there for all to see, don't you think?"

"Indeed, the lad makes a decent point, there is something out there that we are missing. Good work kid but it doesn't stop here, you have to continue searching, and looking and maybe you just might answer the questions that we need to answer". I left the office, headed back for my station when it hit me. I ran back into the office unannounced, and I might have annoyed them, but I wasn't fazed none the less, I had to get to the bottom of this. "What is the problem lad? Seen a ghost or something?" I shook my head to show I hadn't seen a ghost or anything of the like. "What then is the problem?" "Sir I think all the transactions we are seeing are some sort of distractions. Something is going down somewhere, and I think it is devoid of these financial transactions". Ronnie listened with rapt attention but then he responded not as enthusiastically as I would have wanted him to. "Lad, we know something is going down and while you and I are here, checking finances and all of that, we have agents in strategic positions waiting to strike once you have decided that the transactions are strange enough and the top brass at the bureau have decided to strike". The pressure is much for everyone, but I believe we are going to get it right. Something is not right but we will sniff it out".

CHAPTER SIX: IN FRONT OF ME

The final message about a tactical team waiting to strike once I deemed the transactions shady enough didn't give me as much motivation as I thought it would. Having the lives of grown men placed in your hands wasn't as interesting as it did in the movies. The pressure was killing me. I could barely eat, sleep. All I did was go through financial transactions. I had demanded that the intelligence agency pull out the transactions of friends, aides and all associates of Mustapha Al-Aziz. He was doing something, and it was likely he wasn't doing it in his name. I was sure those small amounts transferred to Megatrax had meanings, but I wasn't sure what they meant. I had to keep digging. Life was going away from me. I had myself locked up in a room.

James's bond didn't go through all these in the movies. I was physically lacking and knew I had to go out there, do something. I got up to walk out of my apartment when the phone rang. I picked it up and to my greatest surprise it was the high commissioner on the other end. He spoke with joy when he said, "hey lad, I have some information that would benefit your work". I was excited "what would that be sir?" I responded. He went on "there is an event that I am to attend this evening and I just found out that yours truly Mustapha Al-Aziz is on the guest list. You are clearly not my first choice on a plus one but I'm guessing you need this more than you know. You need the break literally and you also need to see Al-Aziz personally. Maybe you can figure something out". I was super excited, I could try to get how he thinks from looking at him, from being around him but I'd also need to play it super cool, so he doesn't get the slightest idea that I am snooping around. I dropped the phone happily. I rushed into the washroom to clean myself up and look presentable.

What was I going to wear, I ran my hands through all the suits I had in my wardrobe? None seemed worthy of the sort of event the High commissioner was taking me to but a statement my father used to say when I was a kid gave me the confidence to wear what I had. He always said, "it's not the suit but the person that wears the suit". I picked a black one, dressed up looking as smart as I could ever look. I did look like James's bond. It wasn't the kind of mission where there'd be shooting, in fact I hoped there'd be no shooting. I just needed to do a little recon, get information that will enable me to put two and two together to solve the mystery of what Mustapha Al-Aziz was up to.

In thirty minutes, I was ready and as I reached for the doorknob to open it and head out, I heard a gentle knock on the door, "open up sir, it is Anwar" oh Anwar my good friend who wouldn't entertain me with a conversation. I rushed to open the door and saw him looking ever so gentle. He gestures for me to lead the way and I duly obliged. I hopped into the black Cadillac where I met the High commissioner. I was excited at the prospect of meeting top Saudi government officials.

The vehicle starts moving, he looks at me and adjust my tie, dusts off my jacket and says to me "hey lad, don't look so obvious. I know things are moving very fast but try to keep your emotions in control, aye?" I nodded in agreement to the statement. As the car drove, a lot of things were said. We talked a lot about my life, my desires in the service amongst many other things. He told me of his family he had left in England, I was excited. I told him about how I want to serve for a while and get married in Salisbury with a decent woman and start a family and with a smirk on his face he said, "you will do just that son". Time flies when you are having fun they say and in no distant time, we were at the banquet.

We got down from the vehicle and Anwar drove away. When I entered the hall, it was literally like being in heaven although I'd never been. The halls were designed like a palace meant for a king and not just any king, the greatest of kings, like King Solomon or something. The tables were packed filled with decorations, it was a sight to behold, the attendants were all dressed in uniforms and their services were top notch, they got you whatever you ask for regardless of whatever you asked for. I was bamboozled, I almost lost track of why I was there in the first place but thanks to the commissioner who brought me back from my mind trip to the heavens pricking my left arm "remember why you are here lad" I came back to earth, but it was hard to stay focused with all the beautiful goodness that was on display right in front of me.

Dignitaries upon dignitaries kept walking in, it was a ball but the majority of them were putting on a robe and not suits, it seemed different but that was their traditional attire and while I stood admiring the place, he walked in Mustapha Al-Aziz. I looked at him and I must say, he is a rather interesting personality to behold.

Standing at 6ft 1" with short curly hair, round brown eyes and neatly trimmed beards, he had a presence that couldn't be ignored and when he spoke, he spoke with so much grace that I could understand immediately why so many people followed and listened to him, he was in his fifties and looked like he had spent the whole of his life resting in some vacation island or something because unlike a whole lot of the Arabians I had seen, he looked a lot different. His English was even more shocking than his appearance.

He approached the commissioner and in his entourage were a lot of people, one standing out was a man in his early thirties whom he introduced as Mubarak Al-Aziz, his first son, one of two sons he had, the commissioner was receiving him so well like a seasoned actor but here I was looking at him like I could see into his very soul, he didn't take much notice of me but the commissioner did and trying to remove awkwardness, he introduced me as a member of his envoy, Mustapha stretched out his hand and I responded quickly with a bow "it's a pleasure to meet you sir, I've read a lot about you in the dailies", he smiled and responded "you don't say, I hope you only believe the good stuff". We both shared a laugh as both he and the commissioner demanded some privacy as they walked away talking about some issues I didn't know and didn't bother to know. I was left in the presence of his son, Mubarak who seemed very friendly and in no time, we started talking. I was able to find out that he had his degree, masters and his Ph.D. in England at the University of London where he studied Chemistry. I told him a little about myself and we both shared a couple of drinks together.

The commissioner returned shortly after, and Mubarak left. The banquet was celebrating a mutual trade agreement between the UK and Saudi Arabia who had just opened trade for oil. It was the beginning of more trades, but I believed it was a move by the English government to put an eye on Saudi Arabia. Men like Mustapha shouldn't be allowed to believe that wit money, they can do whatever they wanted. There needed to be some sort of check in the world, that would leave the common man with a sense of safety somewhat. I shouldn't be quick to judge, the large outflow of cash form Mustapha's holdings in the UK to megatrax could be purely on business, I couldn't live on assumptions, I had to be sure.

The banquet was going smoothly. The king of Saudi HRH Kazim Adul-Raman of Saudi Arabia was in attendance and gave a speech, it was delightful to listen as he himself also had very good spoken English. It made the place easier for me to stay. As he was speaking, the commissioner spoke to me of a forthcoming event here in Saudi-Arabia that would have the British prime minister in attendance, which he was going to place me in the prime minister's security detail so that I could come in close to Al-Aziz once again. I liked that, it was what I needed, I was on to something, but I needed more time in an around the circle to get the information I suspected. The party after that went smoothly, we had our drinks and left. Anwar took the commissioner to his quarters first before taking me to mine. I went in happy at the prospect that that was a Saturday night, I could sleep in till late on Sunday because I was tired from all the research and the movements. It was true what they say, "mental activities drain you a lot more than physical ones"

I laid down on my couch trying to draw a profile on the personality of Mustapha Al-Aziz, trying to understand how he behaves and if he really is interested in sending weapons into the United Kingdom and even if he were, who was he sending it to? If he was guilty of all these, then the British prime minister would need more security than usual. He wasn't safe but Mustapha didn't look all that suspicious to me. He seemed a regular old man just trying to live his wealth full life in peace but why then was he tagged to so many unsavoury news. I had to keep my head in the game. A lot was riding on my ability to make clear decisions. This was the sort of things I signed up for when I joined the intelligence agency ad, I wasn't going to let anyone down but before that, I needed a drink. I got myself a bottle of scotch, poured a little into a glass, laid back on the couch still wearing the shirt and trouser but no tie and jacket, I started to drink the scotch and in not more than thirty minutes of thinking what next to do, I was already asleep.

CHAPTER SEVEN: PRESSURE

I could barely see anything as we drove through the fog but could hear cocking guns from outside of the car, the sounds of men running towards me and the snapping of twigs like they were running in the bushes. They were clearly over twenty of them from the sounds of the cocking guns, it sounded like they had automatic rifles, I tried to look outside but I could see nothing.

It was a two-way decision, stop the car and get blown to bits or keep moving and get blown to bits, the decision was simple. Keep going and get blown to bits but at least then I had a chance of survival. I wasn't the one driving, it was Anwar, he looked at me and asked me what he should do, and I told him to drive and not stop for anyone "but sir I can barely see a thing", how did I get here? Was the question that flooded my thought, but I needed to change my thinking, how am I going to leave here unhurt was what I should be thinking about. "Don't worry Anwar, we are on the road right, just keep going forward and in no time, we'd be out of here". He nodded in agreement and stepped on it, the car moving fast as we tried to dodge our attackers who immediately opened fire on us.

We were moving fast from what I could feel but it was like they were moving with us; the car was taking massive hits and it was only going to be a matter of time before one of us took a hit. I ducked my head and looked at my side to see Mustapha Al-Aziz sitting next to me with his head in his hand cowering for his life. Anwar was doing what he could, and I had to protect him somehow, I brought out my handgun to return fire but it didn't seem like a wise choice. I mean I couldn't see what was happening outside, who was I even going to shoot at? I'd get hit before I even shoot. I raised my head to give Anwar some sort of moral support just to find out he had been hit by a bullet and the car was without control, I tried to inform Mustapha but before I could say a word we had run into a huge tree, at least that I could see.

I was bleeding and so was he, Anwar was dead but what worried me most was how I got here, why am I in a car with Mustapha and who wanted to kill me so bad? I wanted to do something, but my body wouldn't have it, I don't know why I was in a vehicle with Mustapha, but I was and I had to protect himself. I tried to move but I slowly started to fad out, I tried to say his name or reach for his hand, but I couldn't move. The last face I saw was the pony tailed man I saw at the airport who shut me up before I fainted or so I thought.

I woke up in my room, it was a dream, and I was dreaming but poor Anwar, he didn't have to die. What struck me most was why was Mustapha in my dream, why am I protecting him, isn't he the person I am supposed to be looking for a way to bring down? But biggest of all was who the hell that guy was. First, he shut me up for no reason now he's finding his way into my really bizarre dream, I don't know him at all but I'm really starting to not like him at all. I got up from the couch were I had fallen asleep. I had to stop sleeping on the couch, I was just 21 almost 22 and I was having back aches like I was 60 because I was always falling asleep on the couch and it's not like it's a very big couch, it could barely fit me.

It was Sunday, the only day I had to myself. I needed to do something for myself devoid of work, so I washed up, headed outside to get some things as I needed. There was a convenience store just around the corner, I needed some eggs and milk, I wasn't going to make a cake, but I just needed them. I walked outside; it wasn't that far so I was going to take a walk. I found myself lost in thoughts of work and the dream. Am I going to have to protect Mustapha at some point? Who wanted him dead anyways, I thought he was loved around these parts, the questions kept flooding my mind? It was a dream; it wasn't supposed to mean anything but the pressure from work added to the dream was too much.

I got to the convenience store, picked out what I needed but the thoughts of the strange man hung around me like flies on a carcass. Who was this man, was he among the people shooting at me, did he come there to save me or take Mustapha or worse off kill me? Why in God's name did I faint? Maybe if I had stayed awake, I would have found out who the man was and what his intentions were for me or Mustapha. I was sounding very foolish. A dream wasn't going to tell me the identity of a person. If I needed that information, I needed to work hard for it. I needed to do some digging but I couldn't unless I found out his name or heritage or something.

I paid for my goods and worked out of the store, heading home, I convinced myself that it was the pressure of work that was getting to me. As I walked home, it felt as if I saw that man's face on everybody that passed, if I didn't see the man, I would see Mustapha. I was beginning to become paranoid with the case, but I wasn't going to back down, I didn't mind seeing both their faces on even myself and when I crack this case open and see them on someone else's face, I would point fingers at them and laugh at them. I smiled as I walked home trying to tune down the work madness.

I was living with the pressure of solving the imminent problem using the finances of all parties involved but nothing seemed wrong about them except the sudden influx of small amounts of cash. If there was something wrong, I was missing it. Whoever was involved was very smart and was covering their tracks. Something big was coming, I could feel it, but I couldn't do anything about it. This wasn't the James Bond status I wanted to create for myself, but I had to keep a clean head.

I spend the next three days at the office head down looking at banking details which wasn't telling me anything. Mr Ronnie noticed my countenance and did all he could to brighten me up, but I was more concerned about solving the problems in front of me. The Commissioner had been informed of how I was feeling and how that would affect my productivity and he organized a small get together at his residence. I didn't see the need for it as there was imminent problem before us and we are wasting valuable time drinking and eating. What If before we finish eating, the UK was under attack with the weapons bought from the money I couldn't solve the problems with?

"If you breakdown and die, the bureau would replace you almost immediately. I know Britain is under threat and you are under oath to protect your country, but you have to give yourself a break. I appreciate your effort so far, it's not like you are doing something wrong. If there's something to see, you'd see it lad, I'm sure about that". I was in thought before those words were said, I raised my head and saw the commissioner, Mr James standing in front of my desk. I stood up to salute, but I felt dizzy like there was no blood in my brain. He asked me to sit down and continued speaking "come to the party tomorrow night. Take your mind off work a bit". It'll be fine, it'll work out. We both met Britain in existence and I'm sure we'll die with it still in existence".

With words, he had taken the pressure off my shoulders a little, not that it had been removed completely but I felt good knowing that my efforts had been noticed and appreciated. I agreed to attend the party and rested my head on my desk as he walked away. I couldn't sleep off, but it felt like I was stuck in some sort of limbo, somewhere between the dream world and the real world. I saw my dream play out in my head over and over again. I was trying to in my own way figure out what it meant. I didn't believe in dreams but without answers of any kind, I didn't have any option but to believe in the one that presented itself somehow. I ignored that the fact that the dream asked me even more questions, I felt if I could answer the questions posed by the dream, I could solve all the problems and save my country from any incoming danger.

I knew I had agreed to attend the party but I wasn't up for it, but I decided to none the less. It was the night and I got ready to attend. I got to his residence; this time Anwar didn't come to get me. I got there, it was a small office party, Anwar was there, I felt bad for Anwar, I literally killed the man in my dream, I didn't know if I should apologize to him or something but that would be odd, so I just walked up to him, looked at him and smile. I was going to get that conversation from him this time. "Nice party aye?" he looked at me and smiled back "yes sir, it is". Aha, I had him where I wanted him and just like that, we started talking to each other. My mind didn't completely leave the problem it was going through but for that moment, I focused on the UK I had with me in Saudi Arabia. I had to look out for this one and if I understand true nationalism by protecting the one here, I will know what it entails protecting the motherland. I didn't know if that was the message the commissioner was trying to pass but I had developed a resolve. To protect England, I had to be open to the concept of true nationalism and not just the heroics of being an agent. This was it right in front of me, what I had to look out for.

CHAPTER EIGHT: SCARE

It was a regular morning at work, everyone went about their duties, I was feeling extra happy about my resolve, and the party made me a little closer with my colleagues at the embassy. I came to work that day looking to continue in the mood the previous night and so I did but all our joy was cut short just some hours into work. I was reminded why the only thing I needed to focus in was those accounts. It was like a dream but at that point I realised that not just me but everyone in the embassy with me had passions that burnt for England.

The commissioner rushed out with a paper on his hand, it was a fax, right from the prime minister's office in London. There was a bomb blast at Leicester square. It continues those witnesses were quoted saying that the suicide bomber was Arabic, and he said the words Allahu Akbar before the bomb exploded. The prime minister and indeed all of England were troubled about the incident, I was concerned the most as I knew if I had seen something, this wouldn't have happened. It was a dark day all around the office. I was brought here to Saudi to see first-hand what I needed to solve this case but while I partied all night, people were dying at home. Ronnie knew the progress they made in bringing me back from the dark place I was had been taken over by failure. I went straight for my files; I wasn't going to stop until I put behind bars the person or group of people responsible for the lives lost at Leicester.

I went back to the Ronnie and Col Harry and the commissioner who were sitting together, they say my worry steal the smile off my face from the previous night and that morning. Before I said anything, Harry said "you know it's not your fault, right? There was nothing you could have done about that" I broke a fake smile, with fist clench and the sad feeling of powerlessness, I said "isn't this an attack on the United Kingdom. How are we going to respond?" the men could see my naivety at its peak. "Who are we going to blame for the attack? Until someone comes out to claim responsibility for that attack, it is safe to say we don't know who did it"

I was upset at the way the world functioned, of course we had an idea who did it, and the least we could do was confront him until we got a confession out of him, but these men didn't seem to think that would work. Are we going to sit still and just fold our arms and let the perpetrator of the crime walk away? "We will get through this; this should spore you to play your part and I as well will play my part and everyone will play their part and we will get to the bottom of this". I had one another question to ask, "The prime minister sir, what about the event he has to attend here. Isn't this a statement of intent? Shouldn't we call of that event for safety reasons". "I understand where you are coming from son but I'm sure he'll listen, of course the attack in Leicester was a statement of intent but I know he will come anyways, a stubborn man that one. But have no worries lad, I will talk to him to think and rethink the decision, but I know the most he'd ask me to do is to tighten security".

I wasn't convinced, this was it, they had taken the war to us, and they didn't take it to the barracks, to the marines or the air force, they took it to our wives and children and siblings. That was a cowardly thing to do but I'm sure they are no better than animals and should be treated as such. That day was long and quiet, no one in the embassy made a joke. Silence had taken over and it was accompanied by its brother sadness. Even Anwar who wasn't British felt the pain and agony that swept the entire building. He didn't need to be British anyways to disagree with such antics, he just had to be human.

I stayed away from contact with anyone, trying to whatever I cold to ensure that I bring the terrorists to justice. It was almost time for me to close for the day when Col Harry summoned me into his office. I rushed over hoping to hear some good news from HQ concerning the bomb blast but that wasn't to be, I got in to hear news that didn't seem well to me but would be key in solving this problem. The prime minister didn't change his schedule, he was going to be at Saudi, I was disappointed when I heard it, this was handing our king to them, it was like surrendering your queen in a chase game in a move that had no real positive outcome for us.

Why was he coming anyway? Shouldn't this place be considered hostile already? I felt I was the only one who was thinking straight but at the end of it all, I would find out I was the only one who wasn't. Col Harry had called me into his office to inform me that the prime minister would be coming anyway but that his security detail would be upgraded, that even he didn't know who would be in it. That the English government had pleaded to the Saudi government to allow them carry Interpol as well as having the state security service to the team which the Saudi government had agreed to.

It still didn't sit well to me, we were coming to their home anyways and regardless of whatever security we had, the playing field was theirs to control. This has to be the dumbest decision ever. I nodded, although showing visible disgust to the entire plan, I clenched my fist and uttered a few words under my breath. He smiled as I showed my anger towards the plan, he could feel and see my love for England, which was good enough for any agent to have and not just agents, for any citizen of England to have. As I was about to leave the office, he said to me "telling you that wasn't the only reason I asked you over lad" I stopped and turned around eager to know what was going on, what else could he want from me at this time? "You have been placed as part of the security team". This came as a shock to me, what such an inexperienced agent like myself be looking for in the prime minister's security team?

I wasn't sure how to respond, he continued talking quite as gentle as he always does, I wondered if he wasn't fazed or angry at what just happened at Leicester square? Why was he still this calm? "I reckon you think a lot about what is going on in my mind yeah. I am just as distraught as you are about what happened at Leicester, but one of us has to keep a cool head if we are going to get through this in one piece. I will leave the worrying to you, and I will be calm in dealing with this. I'd rather you try to calm down a little, so you don't get yourself killed before time". I got what he was saying, and I knew he wasn't wrong, I had to learn to not show my emotions every time, I was an agent after all, I had to learn to be strong but it wasn't as easy as he was making it seem but I guessed with time, I'd learn to be like him, cool, calm and collected. He continued "I need you in there as my eyes and ears. I reckon you wonder again why I chose you but then again who could I chose. We are going to use the prime minister as bait to draw out who wants England at their fingertips. It's dumbed I know using the topmost official of the United Kingdom as bait but I'm sure whoever attacked us in Leicester would be swarming over the prime minister like fly to corpse. We've cleared you to be not just in his convoy, but you'll share a vehicle with him".

It seemed a rock-solid plan, risky as it might sound but the sure fire way of sniffing out the criminal. We were using the life of the prime minister as bait but around him, I'd give even my own life to ensure that he is safe. He continued "all that energy and anger you have in you don't waste it, use it to find out who did this and bring that son of a bitch to justice". The urge in me to solve this case just went off the roof. My country was putting its faith in me, and I couldn't let her down. I was going to do everything within my power to solve this. I'll do it where the last words that left my mouth as I walked out of the office. I had been given a chance once more to prove myself and nothing was going to stop me.

CHAPTER NINE: THE ARRIVAL

The day for the proposed summit was fast approaching and every party was getting prepared on their end, I was more eager for the outcome than almost any other person in the entire team of both nations. It was a summit to kick start trade relations between both countries. The UK was going to open trade with Saudi, buying her oil. It was a positive move from both countries economically but what didn't sit right was that some element was trying to hijack the summit and cause tension between both countries. I wondered if they were trying to stop the bilateral trade agreement from being signed or something, but it didn't sit right with me. Signing this contract seemed profitable for all parties involved. Why would anyone want to stop that?

Under these circumstances, I still didn't the need for the UK to agree to the prime minister being here, I mean the High commissioner could sign the document after all, he was the head of Britain's envoy to Saudi Arabia. I knew my complaint would have no real significance to the turn of events as it had already been agreed for him to be here, but I just had to complain to myself anyways. It was three days to his supposed arrival everything seemed right, not even the high commissioner was sure of where he would be lodging. That was the most classified I saw an issue be in my entire years of service, but I understood why and couldn't question. His security detail was seen by only a few so if they were any slip ups, those people would face the full wrath of British law.

My career was just starting but it was starting in grand style. How this ended would go a long way to forging my path for the rest of my years in the service and I wanted a long and successful career, so I was determined to have this go right. I never wanted the worst, I hope for no gun fire of any kind, I just wanted it to go smoothly and for us to have the prime minister out of trouble in next to no time. Three days to his arrival was feeling like seventy years, it was like time paused like one of them avenger movies or something with the time stone. I went about my affairs checking transactions as I get faxed on a daily basis. I knew there was something I was missing, it would be small, but I knew I was getting closer than ever.

I turned up to the office the day before the proposed arrival of the prime minister, it was a day of briefing. The commissioner spent time telling the entire members of staff what this meant to the United Kingdom, it had to go smoothly. He said "I reckon you all know just how important this is for us, the trade agreement will not just allow buy crude from them, it'll also allow us to export our techs out here. We are creating a partnership for the ages, but I believe we all know at the same time that these are sensitive times as regarding the blast at Leicester square. We are all hurting, and we hope and pray that nothing goes bad while he's here. The prime minister for his own reasons opted to be here and I couldn't talk him out of it, so let's do our best to ensure that his time here is safe and eventful". He finished talking and walked out for the rest of us to return to our duties. As he walked away, he signalled for me to follow him which I did, and he asked me if I've been briefed about being in the prime minister's security team? I nodded positively, he continued "I had to do a lot to get you there lad, I knew you needed to be close if you were going to sort out this issue. I am not telling you this to pile your pressure, but I am anyways to make you know that we need you to sort this out and lastly that I trust you can. Godspeed and be safe lad". I felt good that he trusted me, and I had to return that trust.

Work went by quickly and lively, everyone buzzing about the prime minister's arrival. One thing was certain from all the murmuring, no one seemed to understand why he was putting himself at risk coming here. It seemed I wasn't the only one thinking that, but he had made a decision and murmuring about it wasn't going to solve it, we had to do our individual best to ensure that he was fine. I finished all I had to do for the day and went home, as I walked, I admired Riyadh for all it was, I admired the religious and cultural feel that the city brought, I realized what a Muslim could be, they were extremely nice people, that's all I have learnt from my time in Riyadh. That being the case, who is behind the attack at Leicester? How was he any different from all the people I see here? I couldn't understand but why England, what have we done to deserve that?

I got home, and yet again laid down on the same couch that was hurting my back. For someone who was smart, I wasn't exactly smart when it came to the couch. I had something to eat, left over pasta from last night that I had left in the fridge and cold beer to step it down. I had my fill and sat down to go through work stuff, but I don't know if it was excitement or stress from work, but I slept off before I could achieve anything. I woke up hours before my alarm would wake me. I was up, doing nothing, it felt like my adrenaline was over pumping. I was either excited about meeting the prime minister or I was really scared about being in the same vehicle with him as he would obviously be a target. I tried to calm myself down with music, I brought out my recorder and played some records to soothe myself. It was early but not too early for a beer, I got myself a bottle of beer and laid down on the same couch, hoping to fall asleep again but it didn't happen for me this time.

I just laid there anyways, allowing my thoughts to take charge, hopefully I would fall asleep. My subconscious wasn't really interested in helping me that morning, it kept creating images in my head of Leicester square at the time of the attack, even though I wasn't there, it was creating a mental picture. I saw in my head women crying looking for their children, men crying, looking for their wives and children and children crying, looking or their parents and siblings. I saw injured people in my head like I was watching a war movie or something. It wasn't a good sight to behold even if it might not have happened that same way, but it was a spur to keep trying.

It was already 11:00am Saudi time, it was time to go get the prime minister from the Riyadh international airport, I got up, got dressed in my finest black suit, the same one I wore for the event with the commissioner, I was going to meet the most important person I'd ever meet and I had to do that looking as cool, calm and fashionable as I could, I got out the door, after I had done all I needed to, locked my doors and headed for the embassy in a taxi. I got there and the convoy was already set. It was made up mainly the rover p5 vehicle with tinted glass and it would be really difficult to tell one from the other or even tell which the prime minister was going to be in.

I approached Col Harry, who was looking sharp dressed in suit as well, this had to be the most important day of my life, right now as I sat down to remember these events, I would still say it was the most important day of my life, even more than the day of my wedding. I had within me a determination to ensure that all goes well, not that I could control external events should it go bad but even if it does, I was determined to put a stop to it even at the cost of my life. I got into one of the vehicles as directed by Col Harry who was in charge of the security team to pick up the prime minister. I sat down in the front passenger seat eager to meet the prime minister and save the day if necessary.

The drive to the airport was smooth, there was no hitch whatsoever. The driver on the wheels wasn't one I was familiar with, but Col Harry had said he was the one in charge of driving the high commissioner around and that he could be trusted. At that point, anyone who wasn't me, Col Harry, Mr Ronnie and the High commissioner was a threat to national security and couldn't be trusted. I was suspicious of everyone around me at the time. By the time we got to the private airstrip that the Concord (the plane carrying the prime minister) would land, it was still airborne, and the time of arrival wasn't known to anyone, but we prepared the welcome anyhow with security personal offering a guard of honour for the august visitor.

Thirty minutes into our arrival, it was reported that the prime minister was already in site, that he'd be landing soon, he was coming alone with no other British dignitary, that made me a little bit easy as our attention would be completely on him. The plane was right there in our sights, it had landed, and adjustments were made for his welcome, the plane door was open, and the air stair came down, the British soldiers stationed in Saudi saluted for their commander in chief and I as well, stood at attention waiting for my commander in chief as well. It was happening so fast, my career that is, I never expected that in just over a year of my posting to Saudi Arabia, I'd be receiving the prime minister, this was bigger than I expected. I was excited and scared none the less. It had to go well, it just had to be what was on my mind as my eyes gaze upon the prime minister and his entourage, a small group of security personnel as they walked down the air stair. He came down and boy did he look glorious in my eyes, he was your everyday man but to me he was like a god. His grey, white hair laid proudly on his head, his suit the very respect of England, he came down, saluted back at the soldiers who eased themselves, he went straight down to the Saudi envoy who were there as well to welcome him and right there was the prime minister of Saudi Arabia Abdullah Ibrahim Al-Saad and also in his envoy was Mustapha Al-Aziz and his son Mubarak Al-Aziz.

The prime minister being ever so gentle, and kind approached them and stretched out his hand for a handshake to the prime minister of Saudi first and then to Mustapha and lastly to Mubarak. He made a statement that served as a shining light to solving the case once and for all, he said "Mr Mustapha, we meet again and yet again your son is right there with you, I wish my son would care about my everyday affair". The men laughed but I stood there pondering about the statement, his son was always there with him. It was a joke but a statement to be considered anyways, now is not the time I said to myself as the prime minister approached me for a handshake with Col Harry introducing us one after the other.

CHAPTER TEN: REALIZATION

The prime minister when he got to my front, "ah, you must be David Scarlett?" I was shocked at the fact that he knew who I was, I must be doing the right things and, the right things are being said about me. I could barely talk, I was right there in front of the Prime minister of England, I stuttered as I responded "Yes sir!", he smiled and said something only I could hear "I have heard of your love for England and when it was requested that I have you on my personal car, I knew I wanted to meet the man that has been touted to go places in service of his country", I was honoured, I felt very good, I felt like the day should end already, it was already a good day. "Thank you, sir, for the honour, I promise to give my best for my country sir!" with a smile he responded "I trust you will".

When he got the High commissioner, it was like two high school kids who had just seen themselves after a long time, the handshakes, the hugs and the conversation was very friendly. I wondered how someone who had the entirety of Britain to think of could have this much time for a chit chat and laughs but I just settled knowing he was first a human before he became the prime minister. We departed the airstrip in the various vehicles, and I was in the same vehicle with the prime minister and one of his personal bodyguards and the prime minister was way livelier than I thought he'd be. The journey was lively as he went on to tell us tales from his life and times as a politician. We were approaching his residence when he stopped talking for a while and brought up the incidence at Leicester square. Almost the immediately, the smile left my face, he looked at me and continued "that right there is what they told me about, it has been said that you get really emotional when issues concerning England are brought up", I looked at him and replied sir "England is the only home I've got, you don't see English men throwing bombs in Riyadh or any other city in Saudi, I don't know what we did to deserve that, but I will get to the bottom of it and give closure to those that lost their loved ones in the attack". He smiled and said out loud "if every kid in England were like you, it'd be the best place to live in". We all shared laughs until we got to his residence.

I saw in one place more security than I had ever seen in my entire life. The English government was more prepared for this visit than I imagined, I dropped down of the vehicle as well as his security and I rushed for his door, I opened it, he came down with a smile on his face and as he walked inside, he said to me, "you are staying here tonight" I like this kid was what I heard last as he turned forward and walked into the building. I stood out there and watched as all the vehicles drove out of the driveway out of the compound entirely. I joined his personal bodyguard and the both of us walked in. I felt like an actual agent and the prime minister had acknowledged me.

The attack at Leicester was a statement, I had expected some sort of attack on the prime minister's convoy but it was quiet, even at the villa, it was quiet, the prime minister was in a meeting with the prime minister of Saudi, the pair were discussing diplomatic issues which wasn't my business, I just sat down waiting patiently for it all to end. They wouldn't attack now, would they? The thoughts in my head, if they did, they'd be declaring war on both England and Saudi Arabia and that clearly wouldn't be what they wanted.

The deliberations lasted over 5 hours, it was already sunset when the prime minister, his envoy comprising of Mustapha and Mubarak came out of the office of the prime minister, entered their vehicles and drove away. Col Harry approached me and said, "it's going smoothly, I told you didn't have to worry yourself so much, yeah?" I smiled with no reply for that, but I knew I was on to something.

The prime minister summoned me into his office and demanded that I had dinner with him, at first, I wanted to refuse out of courtesy but he insisted and I obliged. It was a full table, the High commissioner and some other top brass staffs at the embassy sat down on the dinner table as they ate their fill. The prime minister spoke to me and asked me about my life. The question came as a surprise to me, but I spoke with confidence anyways telling him every detail of my life. I felt out of place in the crowd but the prime minister made it clear to me that I wasn't, he said with a straight after clearing his voice "you don't have to be in London or in Manchester or in Merseyside or wherever in England to be an English man, wherever you are in the world, as long as you love your country and would do whatever it takes to protect it, you are English and right here on this table, I see only English men. These might be troubled times, but we will make it together". It was a pep talk that made me love England even more.

After dinner, everyone returned to their personal chambers, and it was time for the security personnel to earn their pay. They stayed awake watching over the diplomats as they slept without worry. I hung in the balance; I was neither a diplomat nor a security personnel but I had a role just as important as any other person out there to play. Over the night I kept wondering about Mustapha and his closeness to the affairs of Saudi Arabia, but I convinced myself that since he was an oil mogul, he could stand to gain from the trade agreement with Britain so there was no reason for him to sabotage it.

I slept off that night on a couch as usual. It was calm and silent like every other night, it lasted longer but there was no attack whatsoever. It was day again and everyone was going about their business, preparing for the summit, I got dressed, prepared myself and waited for the prime minister in the rover vehicle. He got in at about 8:50 and we departed the villa for the summit.

The summit like every other thing since the arrival of the prime minister was going smoothly, the trade agreements had been signed by both parties and the British Prime minister gave a short speech after which, the Saudi prime minister gave his speech and the King of Saudi gave his but when it was time for Mustapha's speech, his son Mubarak was the one who talked. His talk was resounding, and people applauded him the loudest. He spoke of his father's desire to support the Saudi government in whatever way they could in ensuring that the trade agreement between Saudi Arabia and England would last for generations and possibly forever. A flashy speech for someone whose father was a suspect of an attack I English soil.

After the summit, the prime minister departed for the villa with his flight scheduled for the morning, that night at the villa, he was visited by the prime minister of Saudi yet again and more deliberations took place after which he turned in for the day. I still felt like I was on to something, but it was a long shot, I just had to hold on to the prime minister was out of Saudi to further those investigations. I had my work file with it, but I was too eager to wait for morning. As the diplomats slept, I pulled up all the file I had on Mustapha and his associates and I was right about something, for someone who was always this close to his father, Mubarak's details and his transactions were absent. He wasn't considered necessary because he had spent all his time in England and wasn't so close to his father until recently. I needed to look at his records and his financial transactions for me to be sure it wasn't a wrong hunch.

I knew I couldn't get access to that information until the prime minister had returned back to England and work had gone back to usual. It was a short night and I found myself drifting off to dream land in the early hours of the day. Almost as soon as I shut my eyes, it was morning again. I had overslept, everyone was almost ready except me. The prime minister approached me as I was clearing out my stuff into my file, he smiled at me, I expected some sort of reproach, but I received a friendly smile, he was about to turn around when he said "good work, lad" and he walked away. I rushed to get set for his departure. It didn't take me time to get set and met him at the vehicle. The ride was as lively as every other I had been in with him and when we got to the airstrip as he was about to board the concord, he turned to me and said with a smile "whenever you get back to England, I'd like to have a cup of coffee with you, yeah?" I nodded positively and said, "thank you sir". He smiled as he walked away and boarded the flight. We all watched the concord take off and I could swear we all sighed with relief that it was over, that he had come and gone without any trouble. It was a good day for us all but for me alone, I had to go back to the office. I had to demand a file. I was on to something, I knew it, but I needed proof.

CHAPTER ELEVEN: ATTACK

Most of the staffs took the day off, the commissioner gave it as a day off, but I wasn't having any of that, I told Col Harry that I was on to something and this was it, this would solve the problem, I was confident, and I knew I had to be. I had to return the trust they had in me by placing me in the Prime minister's security detail. I had seen something; I had seen what they hoped I would see. I got back to the embassy and got close to the computer, I had access to the intelligence files from Saudi Arabia, it was my class D security clearance that allowed me although they were limits to files, I could access with that level clearance. I checked through financial transactions of Mubarak and all the accounts he had in England seemed normal but there was on suspicious movement, it was tied to a Swiss bank account that he was sending tonnes of money into, and I meant tens of millions of pounds. I pulled out the records of that account and it was tied to some Ahmed Fuhad. I didn't know who that was, but this clearly meant something.

I was the only one in the embassy at the time. It was just me and the soldiers who were on duty, I took that information home, waiting patiently for the next day to submit it to Mr Ronnie or Col Harry who would try their hardest to track down Fuhad wherever he was and end this if it was that easy anyways, I was hopeful it was going to be easy. I was happy somehow that I had gotten a step closer to solving this case. Once this is done, I was going to take the prime minister up on that offer of his.

I left the embassy late at night after doing major research to get myself to that point, I got home and laid down on my couch as usual, anxiety having its way over me, I couldn't sleep at all. I just lay down thinking of how much I had grown as a person since I came to Saudi. Yes, I was still awfully emotional as it concerns England but this time, I was dealing my anxiety better, I was drinking soda to sort out my anxiety, I was sleeping better, and I could control my anger preventing mistakes. Adversity really does bring out a man I said to myself. Like a child pumped full of sugar I couldn't sleep.

I was awake till the early hours of the morning. I managed to fall asleep only to see myself in a dream, walking over a completely damaged vehicles with bullet holes all over the car, the occupants definitely would be dead but who was in the car and who wanted them dead so bad, I walked over to the car and saw Mustapha filled with bullets, I looked just outside the car and saw Mubarak holding a rifle, with blood all over his body. I didn't understand why someone so loyal to his father would do that, I tried to stop him, but he ran away. I turned my back unable to catch up to him only to hear the sound of a revolver cocking behind my head, I turned round, and it was Mustapha with a revolver pointed at my head. How is that possible? I just saw him dead with multiple bullet holes in his body, how is he alive and why is he pointing a gun at me? I screamed as he was about to pull the trigger and I woke up at once I started shouting.

It was morning, I got up, washed my face, took a shower, had a bowl of cereal and I left for work with my file, I was so eager to present my superiors with what I just found out about Mubarak, maybe he was the one who funded the attack in Leicester. I got to the office and met Col Harry and Mr Ronnie, I sat them down and gave them details of my findings and it was just what they needed. The suicide bomber was a British citizen by name Ahmed Fuhad and his wife and kids are being investigated as we speak, he wasn't alone on the act, four others were arrested from the basement of his house where they were constructing locally made bombs. It seems England has been infiltrated, there are swarms of jihadists in different parts of the country laying wait to cause havoc. This was it; I have an account tied to Mubarak that transferred a huge amount of money to Fuhad. This was it; he funded the attack. That was the information we need to hold him down. "Congratulations lad, we have with this one but be rest assured, his father will do all he can to ensure we don't take the son so easily" Ronnie said but we have to act now, the High commissioner is supposed to be in a meeting with Mustapha Al-Aziz at this same time. We have to intercept and stop whatever is going there. Col Harry summoned his men and demanded they gear up and get ready for an extraction mission, but Ronnie stopped him at once. "Do you want to start an international incidence; we can't just burst in with guns shooting down anybody that stands in our way".

"We have to hope that he doesn't know we are unto him yet", Ronnie said as he stood up on his seat pacing from place to place. The information was sent back to HQ back in London awaiting orders, but we were asked to stand down for the time being to ensure the safe return of the high commissioner. It was a tensed couple of hours, and it became worse for us as a call came through from

London. A shopping mall in Liverpool had been taken hostage, there were three suicide bombers threatening to blow themselves up if terms were not agreed. What terms were they talking about? What the fuck was going on?

Ronnie at this time was visibly worried, his face had gone pale and his heart beating so loud, I could hear it from across the room, Col Harry being a soldier who the calmer of us but even in his expression, you could tell he was worried, but he had to maintain calm not to cause more than usual scare. Things were falling apart, if only I had realized this earlier, we could have prevented a lot of things. What animal involve innocent people in their deliberations. They could have tabled their terms to the English government as well as the Saudi government and some sort of resolution could have been reached. What did innocent English lives had to do with this?

Ronnie placed a call to Mustapha's villa, to enquire about the safety of the High commissioner and he was told that they both had just left the villa to inspect Mustapha's privately owned refinery and other assets that would be of help to the Saudi government in mass extraction of crude. It was sudden but Ronnie couldn't stay still while all was falling apart, he demands that Col Harry get his men and go in search of the high commissioner while he put a call through to the Saudi prime minister seeking permission for them to be allowed to function. It was going to be hard to get such clearance, but he was willing to use the relationship between both countries as a bargaining chip, he clearly couldn't come along as someone needed to be on sit in the embassy. I opted to go with Col Harry, and he accepted.

I followed the Colonel and his men to the changing room where they got dressed in their complete military regalia, I got dressed myself although not exactly like them, they had on them their Heckler and Koch H11 rifle and I had on me a small berretta 92 handgun. It was my favourite, what I came with from England besides, I wasn't hoping for a shootout let alone a prolonged one. I just wanted it all to end easily, we go over to the site, pick up the high commissioner for safety reasons and bring him back to the embassy awaiting further instructions from London about what next to do.

I might have been a little naïve because the expression on the faces of the marines suggested that they were ready for war. The integrity of England had been challenged and this was the time to show their love for their country. We had finished our preparations when Ronald rushed down to inform us that the office of the prime minister of Saudi had given us its go ahead and that we would get the full support of the Saudi military as well as the police and that they'd do anything within their power to ensure the release of the mall and also see to it that the High commissioner was safe.

Why was everybody sounding like they were sure he was in danger, it could have been as the secretary at Mustapha's villa had said, he might be inspecting assets by now not knowing what was going on at home, we didn't have to be pessimistic, a little optimism wouldn't kill. I wasn't however ready for what would happen next.

CHAPTER TWELVE: RETRIEVAL

We left the embassy in a small convoy, the soldiers weren't much, just about 12 of us. We weren't going there to make a loud bang but a quite retrieval and since it was a case of terrorism, we had the chance to shoot a little if need be, even though I hoped we didn't have to. On the way to the site of the refinery, we saw what shocked us out of pour shell, the Rover p5, official car of the British government that took the high commissioner out from the embassy that morning was lying by the side of the road, saddled with bullet holes. It had been destroyed beyond repair. Col Harry was already too angry to back out now, the rest of his team when they saw his expression knew they were going in for war and had to be ready. Even I knew it had passed the stage of peaceful deliberations, it was an all-out war. We had to get him back if he wasn't dead and if he was making a statement that would remind the terrorists that you can't just met with England and get away with it.

The sight of the destroyed car gave the impression that the attack was fresh, it had just happened so whoever did it was probably still close by and just as we were about to start our navigation by foot to follow the attackers, one of the soldiers was hit on the neck by a bullet. I didn't notice that until I heard Col Harry scream at the top of his voice "Ambush! Take cover everyone", that was when I knew that it had begun, our peaceful retrieval had become a war between nations.

We could barely see our attackers so we had to rely on the sound of their gunfire to return ours, I took cover by the armoured vehicle that we came in. the sounds of bullet raged on like a clash between thunder, it was 1978, but the sounds of automatic rifles raged through the air, the smell of lead and the smell of death came together to produce a stench that wasn't as physical as it was mental. I saw in the eyes of the marines, the desire to revenge, they didn't look like they were afraid of death, their priority was making a statement. I had my eyes gazed on Col Harry as he caressed his trigger releasing stream of rifle bullet and flames came out the barrel of his rifle. He screamed with every bullet as though his screams would increase their intensity, speed or damage. He wasn't alone, the soldiers that were left returned fire. The air was filled with smoke as though there was a bush fire, it was however just smoke coming out the barrels of rifles.

While I knelt down waiting for an opening to return fire, I heard Col Harry trying to rally the troop, he was determined to not give up after coming so close to the kidnappers or killers of the high commissioner, he said "this is it boys, they have our country under siege, our wives, our kids, our brothers and sisters as hostages and they have our commissioner as hostage here. We might be outnumbered but this right here is where we have our revenge, we are going to bring as much of this fucker down as we can, or we are going to die trying". The men seemed ready to continue fire but just as they stood up to continue, the soldier standing right next to me was shot in the chest and as I tried to understand what was going on, his blood poured all over my face like water on a farm. I was shocked and confused, the Colonel however wasn't fazed, his rifle still in his hand as he sent bullet after bullet towards the enemy. "I will run out of ammo pretty soon if this continues", he said. He brought out a grenade from his saddle and threw one into the bushes throwing the terrorists flying into the air. The shooting continued for over thirty minutes and then it calmed down.

The Colonel was cautious of going out of his hiding place, but we couldn't stay like that forever, he had to believe we had pushed them back a little. I don't really think I should say we at this point because I spent all the time cowering in fear, I was afraid, and I didn't shoot a single bullet. I couldn't raise my head up, but he came to me, the colonel that is and said with a smile "you were brave out there lad, don't die on me, yeah? I didn't understand why he was being so gentle with me; I was not a soldier like he was, I wasn't brave like he was, I was a little smart but that was just about it.

We were counting our dead, waiting for backup from the Saudi military, the Colonel called back the embassy to find out the status of the backup as we had sustained casualties and injuries, we had recorded over five dead and two seriously injured. We were already short staffed and pursuing the terrorists would be unwise at this point. Ronnie on the other end was quiet, not willing to spill more bad news, Harry noticed that Ronnie who spoke normally with so much power was hesitating. Something was wrong "tell me Ron, I can take it, what is going on?" Ronald hesitated but had to say it anyhow, however. "We are under attack in three fronts lad" Harry was confused "what do you mean?" Ronnie continued, "Your backup is under attack as we speak, and your squadron might have even more integrity than they do. They took major hits and recorded over seventy percent dead. It's not looking good at the moment. It seems you are on your own for the now". Harry clenched his rifle tightly as he uttered curse words under his breath, but he wasn't willing to stop now, he was going to chase the mission to the end.

Harry looked at his squad or what was left of it, he felt sad about what he was going to do next, but he was going to do it anyways. "I know this is not what we are about, but we have to keep moving. Those of you who can move, stand up and move with me. Those who can't, please stay safe until we complete this mission, we will be back for you". He said these words with so much heaviness on his heart, I looked at him and I could swear I saw tears dropped from his eyes and rolled down his cheek, he refused to wipe them so that his men won't see that their fearless general was just a man like the rest of us and could cry.

I was in over my head, but I wasn't going to stop now, we definitely were close and the next time it happened, I would be more than ready to defend my country. I never expected us to get the go ahead to shoot at them in another country but since it had been gotten, what matters most is the integrity of Britain. The US had just lost a war at Vietnam the year before. I didn't know much about that and didn't concern myself, but we weren't going to lose this fight. I picked up a rifle from one of the dead soldiers, brought out the cartridge, checked how many rounds it had left, I knew I was going to do this.

Col Harry looked at me with a smile on his face, he had something in his mind that he wanted to say to me. I didn't know what it about me was that these men found so interesting, I wasn't half as brave as any of the soldiers that just died saving their country. I didn't think I had the needed conviction to do what they did but they saw in me something I didn't see in myself, what was it they saw, I needed to see it for myself. He walked to me, placed his hand on my soldiers and said to me "this is not what I want from you in this mission. The place would be laced with terrorists, and we are not sure about back up yet, I need you to do one thing for me however".

I would do anything for him, like his men, I was willing to follow him to the depths of hell and back, I just needed him to say the word, "you are not going in with us", I would do anything else but not leave them now when they needed me the most, I didn't understand what he was asking of me, "I can't go back now sir, I signed up for this, I'm one of you aren't I?" he smiled as he responded "I am not asking you to go back, what I am saying is, the route I and my men are taking is one that doesn't guarantee our return and in light of that, you can't follow us in. I have a mole in Mustapha's arrangement for a while now, he's not in on Mubarak's plans but he has a heads up on where they are. He's going to send coordinates soon and we'll be there to intercept them. I need you to go with him. Our squad is too big to go in for the rescue, we are going to grab their attention and give you enough time to sneak in and save the high commissioner. We are not sure yet if Mustapha Al-Aziz had been kidnapped as well but if he has, save him too".

The day was clearly not how I thought it would be, my big break into the intelligence agency was claiming too many important lives. My very first mission had involved dead English at Leicester square, had involved the kidnap of the high commissioner, marines had died, more hostages had been taken in England and now Col Harry and his entire team would die just so I could swoop in, make the rescue and look like the hero? This wasn't how I thought it would be, I thought I could save everybody but that was just not possible, I wasn't thinking straight, I was just being a kid, I had to grow up now, I had to man up and do the right thing.

CHAPTER THIRTEEN: ALONG CAME THE SPIDER

I agreed with the plan as it didn't seem like he was going to back down from that, I carried weapons and ammunitions as I could, my trusted berretta 92 at my side, I crossed the automatic rifle over my shoulder and bade farewell to the Colonel who signalled his men to move forward. He has hand signals and they moved quietly to a camp. It looked like some sort of abandoned village of some sort. It had small buildings up to like twenty and to think it laid just beneath the small forest we just passed. The colonel knew to steal their attention, he had to make an entrance that they couldn't ignore, and we all hoped in our hearts that this was where they were keeping the commissioner hostage because if it wasn't, we might just have reduced his chances of being kept alive. I knew it was in all our minds, but nobody wanted to be the bearer of bad reports, so I kept quiet myself.

He signalled his team to approach from the east end, before they left, he looked at me and said "you are on your own now lad, I trust you'd make the right decisions, yeah? He'd join you once you're in. meet him on the south end before searching for the final hide out". "But I don't know who you are talking about, how would I know if I see him?" he looked at me and with a smile, he said "you'll know and if you don't, he'll know". That wasn't very assuring, I was going to risk my life with someone, I should at least know who he is, what if I walk into one of the terrorists and assume that he's the one only to have my English arse shot while I look away.

I waited patiently for the grand slam entrance of the colonel, we had no back up, five of us are going into a terrorist camp to do the same work that would take a whole garrison of soldiers to achieve plus I was getting help from a mystery man. I was muttering to myself, I heard a loud explosion and I looked towards the direction where the sound came from and saw a mushroom of smoke go up high into the air and almost at once, I heard shouts and footsteps followed, running towards the direction of the explosion and multiple gunshots followed.

As I laid there waiting for the footsteps to stop coming so I can sneak into the camp, the noise of gunfire sent thoughts through my mind, I held tightly my rifle as I imagined the reactions of human body receiving hot lead bullets moving at supersonic speeds. I saw in my minds eyes the courage four marines had to take on an entire squadron of terrorists, I couldn't let them die for nothing, I had to sneak in, rendez vouz with the asset, make a swift retrieval and head out ASAP. When I could no longer hear the footsteps of people running, I sneaked into the barracks and headed for the south wing as I was told to do. Like a ninja, I tried to avoid all possible confrontations with anyone.

I find my way through the small buildings, avoiding the windows just in case any one of them did not feel the need to go out to shoot at the invaders. I laid low, crawling on the floor where necessary, I found out I wasn't as discreet as I thought I was when I heard in a hushed tone "what are you doing? I have been waiting for you for a while". I got up a little, not enough to be seen but just enough to get a clear view of who was talking to me, it was the pony tailed guy I saw at the airport, yes, the one that shut me up, I look at him, this was it. Maybe he came to save me in my dreams. My dream was beginning to pan out. I will be saving Mustapha and he'll be saving the both of us.

I had a lot to talk to the guy about, but I had to wait for a better time and that time clearly wasn't now, we had to do what was in front of us before I talked personally with this man. "What is the plan?" I asked him as I ensured we were not being watched. His response was shocking almost as much as the situation we were in "I thought you had one, aren't you the agent with the brains and all?" I shook my head and said, we just have to find out where they are, make our way in, shoot a couple of people and walk away at the right time.

He smiled and asked me to follow him, "I have been here a while, I have an idea where they took them to, I'm not sure they are still there but I saw them go in, its heavily guarded and we'll need to be at our very best if we are going to go in and out. What is the status on backup he asked?" I responded by shaking my head, "So we are on our own? Typical" he said as he ran towards a building. All the time he ran, he was docked down to avoid being seen. I followed him closely.

He assumed higher grounds, pulled the bag behind his back and told said "this is where we earn our pay" he brought out a gun in pieces, he was having a casual conversation with me as he assembled his rifle, from nothing, he had an L42A1 sniper rifle and he placed its 7.62×51mm cartridge and from nowhere, he had a sniper rifle, he laid down on the floor and said to me "I'd advise you either take cover or head towards that house over there and take advantage of the commotion that I will cause right about now". Taking cover seemed the smarter choice but I was tired of having people solve my problems, so I headed for the building and just as I was on the window, he shot one of the soldiers in the head and as the second soldier rushed out to locate the shooter, I hit him hard with my rifle and he dropped. I looked at him, I didn't have to kill him, my partner works over and I wanted to address him but he hadn't said his name, while I tried to sort out what to call him, he borough out his knife and slit the throat of the soldier I had knocked out. "You didn't have to do that, he was already out", he smiled and said, "don't be naïve kid, if it were you, he'd have done the same and my name is Hassan".

You don't have to stay here mourning your enemy David, let's move on, there's more of them, we are going to have to engage them eventually but for now, let's reduce confrontations to a minimum. We continued on our stealthy exodus and Hassan like a ninja quick to take the life of any terrorist who missed as his little as his scent, he was a cold-blooded killer. Who was the mystery man I was walking with? He made it a little easy, but I couldn't rely on him forever, I had to make my presence felt. I was new to all this, but this was the life I chose, and I had contribute somehow to the mission. The Colonel trusted me, and I have to return his trust.

We left a trail of corpse as we went into the building, the building looked really small on the outside, but it looked like we had been walking for at least ten minutes, we had entered a tunnel that lead to some underground lair or something. We got close to a door, and we heard words "you are weak father, I never expected you to be creating alliances with them, you are bringing them right to our very doorsteps and the next thing, they'll condemn the very essence of Islam. You know they are like viruses, they start, and they spread". "You don't have to do this Mubarak, you'll start an international incidence and lots of people will die son, you can stop now". "Yes boy, you can stop now, you don't have to go any farther than this, I will put in a good word for you, and it wouldn't be that bad" another voice said. That was James Perkins, the High commissioner, I was sure that was him.

We have to go in there, we have to save them both, my dream was paying out but this time, I wasn't the one who needed saving, I was going to be doing the saving. "Don't be rash lad, we will save them both, but we can't go in guns blazing" what was he talking about? I've seen him go all commando on these guys, now that I need him to actually Chuck Norris these fuckers, he was talking about not being rash. What happened to all that Ninja stuff? He was clearly more experienced on the issue at hand, so I waited patiently for his next move. The dialogue continued "I watched you associate with them all your life, you sent me to school and live with them, infidels and now you want to bring them back to Saudi? I'd rather die and watch that happen".

The high commissioner cut in quickly "this is an issue we can sort out ourselves, you don't have to hold hostages in London". "You think I don't know this place is already been taken over by your marines?" They are my bargaining chip out of here. If anything happens to me, they'd die. Right about now, I know this place is already surrounded. You didn't expect me to live my escape in the hands of chance, did you? Once I call my brothers over at England and give the say so, they blow up the place sending countless of those infidels to their early graves. They'd be blessed beyond words. It's a chance we have to take to rid the world of infidels" "I never raised you to be an extremist Mubarak, I sent you to school abroad to appreciate the ways of others. Life isn't the way you see it. With this trade relationship, we can bring our people and theirs together and open way for a better life for a lot of people. You don't have to kill innocent people; I guarantee you that you won't feel good when you do". Mustapha tried to warn his son. "Shut up! Father, you have gone soft from all your associations with them, you have missed it all. I am not very proud to be your son right about now. I hope you repent and make peace with your maker and find your place in Allah's good books".

The dialogue continued for a while and when all parties had a pause to rethink their stance, Hassan snuck in the open door. We had managed to keep ourselves hidden. The mission had been made a lot easier, kill Mubarak and the jihadists in England will not have any order to go by, allow him to live and risk the lives of countless English. It was not a choice. I'd kill Mubarak over and over. He was a heartless killer, lives meant anything to him. Hassan already snuck into the room, he was hiding behind a table, waiting for the right time to pounce at Mubarak but it would be tough as he had two others in the room with him, a gunshot also would attract those that were outside.

Sweat rolled down my face as I pondered the best course of action, what we would do to make sure the high commissioner and Mustapha Al-Aziz were safe. It had to be the priority at the moment, but we were at a disadvantage. Time was ticking, Mubarak wasn't completely convinced he wanted to kill his father, he was fighting a battle with himself, but he knew what he didn't want and that was obvious, he didn't want British involvements in Saudi Arabia. He would do all he needed to kick us out. I couldn't think of what to do, I looked at Hassan who looked like he had run out of ideas as well. He gestured that he was going to just charge in damn the consequences. If we could take them down, we could use Mubarak as bait for our escape but that was too risky. One of his henchmen could easily just call his team and blow off the mall in England.

I couldn't say it was a miracle as despite my six months with the good bishop, I wasn't much of a religious person but just as Hassan was about to go out guns blazing, a chopper probably belonging to the UK embassy or Saudi military flew over. It was the Boeing Vertol YUH-61, an amazing war vessel and it rained bullets like rain on the terrorists that had remained in the camp. It was clearly heading for the fighting soldiers on the east end of the entrance, but it gave us the opening we needed.

Mubarak and his fellows were distracted by the sound of the chopper and Hassan came out from his place of hiding, shooting the two men close to Mubarak before being shot himself by Mubarak and at the same time, I shot Mubarak on the arm holding the gun and he dropped the gun on his arm, he wanted to pick it up again with his left arm and I shot him again making it impossible for him to pick up either the gun or the phone. I got close to him, knocked him out with my barrette handgun and he fell to the ground.

I untied both men quickly and head to where Hassan was lying in a pool of his own blood, he had something to say but he was too hurt to say them, I wanted to put pressure on the bullet wound to give him enough time for medic to show up, but he was hit on the neck. He was bleeding form the bullet wound as well as his mouth. I looked at him, a half smile rested on his face. I had seen too many associates die and risk their lives, he held me close as he tried to say some words, but nothing came out. I could feel life slip out of him; I'd do anything to give him life but here was nothing I could do. He didn't answer my questions and the most important of which was why an Arabian was fighting on the side of the British? I looked at Mubarak who was struggling to get up and by the time I looked back at Hassan, he had passed away with his eyes open. I closed them, walked to Mubarak and apologized to Mustapha before I started landing blows after blows on his idiot son. For someone so full of prospect, he had wasted his life living on some idiot ideas that some were infidels while others were fighting a religious war. Didn't he learn anything from all that school he had attended? He fell on the floor again, his eyes swollen as blood trickled down his lips, nose and forehead. That wasn't enough but I wanted to inflict as much damage as I could. By the time, the shooting outside had stopped, I picked up a rifle, asked both men to stand behind me as we heard footsteps heading for the underground room that we were.

If by the time, they came down and it was enemies, I would take as many as I could with me down to hell, but it wasn't, it was members of the Saudi military. Boy, was I glad to see Arabians. They rushed over and took the men out, I hurried out hoping to see Col Harry and his men still standing but that wasn't to be. They held the entrance long enough to allow us in and for some sort of back up to arrive, but they didn't make it. The sight of the lifeless body of Col Harry on the floor brought tears to my eyes. Friends, associates all gave their lives for what they believed in. That was the basis on which I'd model what is left of my career in the service. I'd die protecting people, it didn't have to be just English lives, and whatever life I could save was worth saving.

CHAPTER FOURTEEN: RETURN

The mission was a success at our end, the suicide bombers were thwarted and in MI6's custody, but it didn't feel much like a success to me. I had been in Saudi just over a year and I had made a lot of friends and I had lost a lot of friends. It was September of 1978. Staying in Saudi Arabia didn't feel right to me anymore and rumours had it that I would be reposted on special recommendations. Two weeks had passed since the incidence, I saved lives but why didn't I feel as good as I thought I would be? I was sure James's bond didn't feel this bad at the end of every movie, if he did, he wouldn't last as long as he did in the service.

I was at the office when I was called to the High commissioner's office, he looked at me with pride as he said to me "I know you fell off for the numbers of friends you lost out there that day, I want you to know as I know that Harry believed in you as did I and he would be very proud of you for what you achieved. You are going places in the services and its high time you believed in yourself. I don't know how you'd react about the news I am going to give you know but you have been reposted back to London, you are to resume at the GCHQ by Monday. It is important to note that this was a request made directly by the prime minister. Your efforts had been noticed and the higher ups are recommending you for this honourable job. God speed lad, it was a pleasure working with you".

I met the news with indifference. Regardless of where I go, Saudi Arabia would always remain in my mind, it gave me the experience I needed to grow up and become a man. I was conflicted about the meaning of success however as I was sure this was not the feeling that went with winning, but I had to accept that to win a war, you have to lose some battles. I had five days to clear out my table and clear out my apartment.

I went home on the day not displaying the emotions of James Bond like I thought I would have while I serve in the agency. As I cleaned my beloved berretta, I wasn't sure of what was next, but I thought in my heart that nothing would top the experiences I had here. I clearly didn't know where my secret service life would lead me to next.

December 25, 2006

I was brought back to reality when my friends who were so engaged with their drinks and the game on TV screamed, I jumped off out of my slumber, and it seems I had spent a major part of the night remembering about the start of my journey in Saudi Arabia. It was getting late, and I had to go back to Carla's parents to have what was left of dinner with my wife and her family. My memories had reminded me a little of how much we should hold those dear to us, we never know when it'd be our last. I was a 61-year-old agent, I wanted to be reactivated but it wasn't happening yet, I had to live what was left of my life.

I excused myself as I head on home to Carla's, by the time I got there, she was having dinner with her parents with an expression on her face that suggested she was far from happy, and I wasn't doing my best to make her happy like I vowed I would. This woman had stayed with me throughout the majority of my year in service, the lies I told her constantly to allow me to go about my missions. I was sure at some point that she knew I was lying but she didn't challenge me too much about it. When she saw me, she got angry and started to cuss at me, but I approached her and hugged her from behind. I'm sure she was confused as to why I did that, but I didn't need to explain to anyone why I hugged my wife, she was shocked and returned the hug, she turned around and held me closely. "I don't know if we can spend the night here" Mark, Carla's father said yes, and we both headed for Carla's old room. The bed wasn't much but we would manage it, I could see in her peace like I had not seen in a while. She held me close as we both shared her small bed.

In a short while, Carla was asleep, I couldn't fall asleep, and I just stared at the ceiling as I fell back into my remembrance.

March 5, 1978

When I arrived in London from Saudi Arabia, it was blissful, the thought that I had returned home, I could continue for a while here while I await any new posting, but I was swung back into action quicker than I expected. I got back home, dropped my bag, had a bath and slept a long while. My father and my mom just kept their eyes fixed on me. I was clearly a different person from the David that left home, I had grown up, but they were sure I hadn't grown up under the right circumstance. They however tried their best to make me feel at home.

The next day was the mass burial for all the marines that had lost their lives in Saudi, and I wouldn't miss it for anything. I had to pay my last respects to Col Harry and Hassan. They were the true heroes; I was just an overly dependent cry baby. If I had manned up, maybe they wouldn't have died but I couldn't draw myself back. I had to become a better man and an even greater agent via their sacrifices, it was lives second chance to me to prove my worth and I wasn't going to let either of them down. I stood at the back, trying to hold back my tears as I saw the widowed wife and child of Col Harry. After the burial, I went to her with tears rolling down my cheeks, I saluted her, and she began crying all over again. I hugged her, knelt down before his child and told him that "your daddy, was the greatest man I ever saw, I know he is in heaven watching over all of us right now. Don't be sad, yeah? He lives in you". I said pointing at his chest.

All fallen soldiers were given a medal of honour at their funeral with their wives, kids and brothers receiving them on their behalf. I wasn't a soldier and didn't receive any, however I got the biggest reward of all. I had my life. After the funeral, I was summoned to GCHQ where I met with the deputy director, who informed me that I had received a special posting, I was posted directly to the personal security detail of the prime minister. He sounded surprised himself when he said to me "I reckon you did really well for yourself because recommendations were flying everywhere for you. We had to listen to the most important one and that was the prime minister himself requesting for your posting to his security detail". I was confused and I had to respond anyhow "is protecting the Prime minister the job of British intelligence?" he laughed when he said, "when top brass demands you lad, you go, that is how we serve". I wasn't sure about the prime minister's personal security detail, but I was going to serve my country anyways I could. I excused myself from his office as I walked home tired like I had been in a farm all day.

CHAPTER FIFTEEN: A NEW CHAPTER

I had been with the prime minister some months now and all seemed so well, there was not much to worry about in terms of security, he had a special interest in me since we met in Saudi Arabia, I wouldn't lie, I enjoyed his company a great deal. I was learning a lot from his personally and politically. He was letting me in on almost every state dealing he had. That wasn't right I agree but we had attained that level of trust for each other. I was basically family, he treated me not just like an agent in his security detail but like an adviser, it was a rather easy posting. I was 23 at the time and I was having the time of my life.

It was about the same period that I met Carla, a beautiful young woman aged 20ma, she was trying to find her path in life, I met her at a coffee shop in one of my morning rush for work, I was up late and had to rush down to get a cup of coffee, I was looking so tired when she offered me coffee, I could swear, she said more than just my name as she offered me coffee because my ears and my heart heard something more, it was like she called out to my heart. Her voice was soft, her long curly hair, stretching up to her lower back, he blue eyes rested gently on her forehead and her pointy nosed poked its beautiful edges at me. She had lips, small but pleasant and she smelled gently like the oceans breeze. I knew I had to come back for more coffee over and over again till I could talk to the lady.

I was in a good place with work, I could see myself settling down, spending the rest of my life with her but I had to get to work first that morning because if I didn't have a job, marrying her would just get complicated, we both couldn't rely on the income she makes from the coffee shop. As she offered me the coffee, I stuttered but mustered courage to ask her name which she told me was Carla, "Carla ei? I am David, David Scarlett, I am really eager in staying here and having a long conversation with you but I'm sure if I do that, I'd be working with you at this coffee shop, not that I'm saying its bad working here but I have to go back to work. I do hope to meet you here again". She had a smile on her face as she agreed and watched me run away so fast towards work. She let out a gentle smile and chuckled as I sped off heading straight for work.

Over the next couple of weeks, I went to the coffee shop where she worked every day for my morning coffee, it became a ritual, all I did to meet the girl of my dreams. I wonder where all that went wrong, it's been years, but I still believe she is the love of my life. I even told the prime minister of England about her, and he gave me his advice. I never expected my life to take this route, I thought I would serve quietly for a while before I'd be deactivated towards the latter end of my life, I didn't think my service would lead me to the love of my life and bring me close to the prime minister of the country I love so much. I had earned the nickname invincible man from my time in Saudi Arabia. It was borne out of the fact that out of everybody who went out to rescue the commissioner, I was the only one that came back, they said I was invincible and swept in and out of the den of terrorists not realizing themselves how many sacrifices were made for me to come out on top. I couldn't stand to explain the situation, I couldn't put myself through the pain of talking about those times, so

I accepted the name anyway. It made me sound mysterious somehow.

It was like my life had fallen out of a really stiff James Bond movie and its now in a romance, I was blushing way more than I was wiping sweat off my face like I did in Saudi Arabia, I was hanging out at coffee shops more than I was sitting in front on my desktop in Saudi Arabia, I was going out a lot more than I did back then as well. It was like the dark feel of life associated with the dangers I went through had been replaced with so many bright colours, like it was no longer darkness and sorrows, it was now rainbow and flowers. Carla and the prime minister had almost made me forget friends that I lost while in service although it would be impossible to forget their sacrifice and I would often have nightmares, but I was doing really well at the moment, and I wanted it to continue like this. Nobody gets this happy and wants to go back to anything that reminded them of their sad past.

I found myself focusing more on Carla and my personal relationship with the prime minister. I never thought one person could go through so much in their life as I did over the past two years of my life. I knew the events in Saudi Arabia would prepare me for what to face in my life going forward but it did forge in me a complete love for my country. What I was going to meet next was going to cause a great divide in my loyalty to my country, but one thing remained, I did what I felt was right and I was sure in my heart it was right even though it caused me a lot of pain.

I wished my life would continue down this path however, that I would continue being this happy, Carla was all I wanted at the moment, she gave me listening ears whenever I needed it, she would be my peace whenever I came back from work stressed or tired. I was spending more time in her coffee shop than I was in my own home, but it was worth every moment, looking at her face could take my mind away from all the stress of the day and physically reset my stressed muscles. I knew that was just the loving working, but I didn't mind being delusional for this woman. I did all I could to get her to go out with me, but she made it really hard for me. Despite my intelligence and ability to do all sorts of intelligence work, espionage and all that, I couldn't break through the defence systems of a woman. She made me wait and search and pursue her and it made me want her a lot more.

It was a Friday morning on my way to work, I dropped by her coffee shop, I saw her again, attending to a customer with her hair falling just over her face, I couldn't hold my feelings in check anymore, I cut lines with everybody there snarling at me as I walked to the counter. I got there, looked at her unable to utter words, she raised her head and with her left hand, she gently moved her hair from her face to her ears so she could see me properly. I just had to say it anyways, in the presence of everyone I asked, "I'd like to take you out to dinner sometime, any time". She clearly was shy but I saw in her that she appreciated the gesture, she was visibly blushing "not now, let's have this conversation later" I was going to respond when someone from the crowd screamed "answer him so we can get our coffee, we have our jobs to get to and he doesn't look like he's going away until he gets an answer", there was a chorus laughter from everyone waiting for their morning coffee. I wasn't the guy for grand gestures, but I knew that guy had just done me a favour. She looked at me and with a smile on her face, she said OK. "Tonight by 7". I didn't know who the guy was that made that statement, but I was really grateful for his help. I walked out of the coffee shop without my coffee, but I felt a lot better than I have in a while.

CHAPTER SIXTEEN: CONFLICTED

Work that day went by slower than usual, nothing made sense, all that came to my mind was sitting down at dinner with Carla, and I couldn't tell if she was feeling this same way, or I was just being overly excited. She had managed to be really cool about my whole interest, but I was out here doing the most. I had to play it cool, but I couldn't. I had never really noticed a woman like this my whole life. I had focused more on my studies and improving myself so I could become the best at my job, but she was a distraction, one that I approve of.

I went about my duty not wanting to have any reason to stay behind after work, I needed to clear my desk and my head and have one thing in it for the rest of the day and that was Carla. I was summoned to the Prime minister's office, he had work to discuss with me and I rushed in as I didn't like to keep him waiting for any reason, he looked at me and could see from my expression that something was making me excited. He placed the work on hold and asked me why I was so giddy "I responded like a child who had good grades in school and was in a hurry to tell their parents at home. "I finally got her to go out with me". He smiled and was visibly interested in the details of my adventure into the heart of the lady of my dreams, but we had to discuss some important work issues. "What was it you wanted to talk to me about?" I asked ready to go about that duty as well to clear my schedule completely for the night, but he brushed it off by saying "no need for me to bore you with work, it can wait, you can take the rest of the day off to prepare for your big date"

I knew something was up, but he didn't want me thinking too much about it, I thought to myself as I walked out of his office, what could be wrong, I hadn't seen him like this in a while. I wanted to help him out, but he wanted to do me a favour, I thought to myself, first thing in the morning, I would rush back to work, receive the work briefing from him and if possibly tell him the outcome of my date the night before. I walked away not knowing what to think of the Prime minister's countenance but knew in my heart that it'd be ok.

It was 5:15pm, I walked home alone, I wasn't as excited about my date as I was in the morning. The issue at the prime minister's office clearly had me thinking. What issue could he be in, whatever it was, I knew I had to do my best to help him out of it. I brushed these thoughts to the side; I was overthinking things yet again. What problem could the prime minister of England be in that I could solve. I was just a lowly ranked agent; I don't even have the security clearance to find about such issues. I just smiled as I walked towards my house. Carla had given me her address to pick her up, she asked me to be there at 6:30, I had an hour and 15 minutes to be ready, I needed to look my best, I was trying to impress this lady, and she was clearly the girl of my dreams.

I got home, tried to prepare myself for the date but all the while, my mind was still right there at Downing Street with the prime minister. What was he going through? How was I going to help him? I dragged myself through the entire preparation and in no time, I was done, the time was 6:15. I left my home heading for Carla's parents' house. I got there 5 minutes early and I knocked gently on the door, it was opened, and I met a man standing there, looking at me, obviously it was Carla's dad. I ought to be scared somewhat but I seemed a little uninterested. I greeted him however and he replied calmly "I am David sir", he nodded his head "I reckon you are here for Carla?" and I nodded as well. "Well come on in son", he said with a smile, I was glad he was gentle with me as I was almost not here mentally "this is my wife, Laura". I looked at his wife and found out where Carla got her beauty from, Laura although in her forties could pass as a twenty-year-old, she had long flowing hair and a pointy nose as well, and she hadn't aged at all. I'd have believed she was Carla's sister if I was told.

I looked at Carla's mom and finally I said "nice to meet you ma'am, I must say you look lovely" she covered her mouth as she smiled a little. Mark cut in jokingly "looking to take my wife as well as my daughter away, yeah? What have I ever done to you lad?" We all shared a laugh.

I sat down on the couch waiting for Laura when I saw her coming down the stairs, I was dumb founded, and her parents looked at me the whole time as I had my mouth open and my eyes watery as I beheld beauty in its purest form. She wasn't dressed in anything to fancy neither did she have much made up on, but she stunned me. I could feel my heart pound, I could hear my heartbeat in my ears. She was fair and her beauty could put Marilyn Monroe to shame. I looked at the wanders of God's creation in one being. As she walked down the stairs, I felt so proud that all that beauty was coming down just to meet me. Her long flowing hair had been brushed ever so gently and tied in a sort of ponytail, she had lip gloss on that was bright red and it made her eye colours pop out, he teeth shined so white and her skin ever so delicate.

Words usually fail me when I was excited and all but right now, I was beholding a beauty that didn't just take away the words from my mouth, it took them from my brains as well, I tried to compliment her when she got down, but the right words to use weren't forthcoming. She wasn't offended, everyone there knew I wanted to say something, but I was caught under the trap of her beauty. She smiled when she approached me, "you can say anything you want, it's okay", and I just looked her in the eyes when I said "you have redefined beauty to me. You are an angel clearly, I just wished you'd be my own angel". It sounded corny to me, but it meant something to her, she blushed uncontrollably and tried not to make eye contact with me.

Her parents didn't want to intrude but I knew we had to go for me to be able to bring her back in time, her dad looked at his wife in an awkward silence and said "this is our queue to live you two alone, if you need us, we'd be in the kitchen", I smiled as I stretched out my hand for a handshake "thank you very much sir", he smiled back as Carla and I headed for the door. The night was already going perfect, but I had to make it better. I walked her out of the door and like a gentleman, I opened the door of the car, we enter the Ford Cortina, it was my father's car, but he allowed me to borrow it anyway. He knew I had to make this night perfect.

We went to a restaurant not too far from her home. We started talking about our lives, she was an only child, and she was currently studying in school. She was cheerful and told me a lot about herself without any restriction, I knew at this point that the feeling was mutual, she probably liked me as much as I did her. She noticed I wasn't my usual chirpy self. She was self-conscious and she asked, "did I do anything wrong?" I was shocked why she'd think that I responded immediately "you didn't, tonight couldn't be any better than it currently is". "Then why are you not happy?" was her response. I knew she had picked up from my countenance that I was down, and I had to liven the place. I used my hand to move the strand of hair hanging in front of her face to the side of her face so that I could look at her yet again and it was quite the sight to behold.

I tried to brush off the issue by saying "it's just work stuff. It's nothing to bother about". She knew it wasn't, but she wasn't going to push. I liked that about her, she knew when I needed to space and also when she needed to be in my space the night was perfect. I had talked to her, and I knew that she clearly had interests like I have. We spent the rest of the night talking about our dreams, where we wanted to be in 20 years and a lot that we said were similar. I knew in my heart that she was the woman for me, but I needed to know if I was the man for her.

It was the best night of my life yet but like every goof thing, it had to end, it was ten already and I had to take her home even though I didn't receive an order to bring her, I just felt it was right. I drove her to her father's, I parked in front of the house, I walked her to her door, she turned back and looked at me, she was still beautiful to me even though I've been looking at her the entire night, I just couldn't get enough of her. She was about to walk into the house, but I wasn't having any of it, I had been fighting myself all night if I should kiss her after the first date. I held her hand, pulled her towards me, with my eyes closing as my head moved towards hers, I had poked my lips with the intention of kissing her, but she stopped me with her index finger. Not so soon tiger, she said as she freed herself from my grip and went inside, before she locked the door, she looked at me, came out and kissed me on my cheek and said a beautiful goodnight.

I was conflicted with myself now on so many fronts, first off, what was going on at work, then attempting to kiss her and being turned down. Maybe it was a mistake, the latter was a pleasant thought as I wondered what was going on, but the former was a genuine concern. My distraction was gone, I had returned to my worries. What was it that I had to be told? I needed to find out, once I get to Downing Street the next morning, I would rush into the prime minister's office to find out. I couldn't sleep that night as I stayed awake wondering what it would be that he had to tell me.

CHAPTER SEVENTEEN: CHANCE

I got to work the next day to hoping to find out what he had to tell me, but he brushed it off to the south saying "it was all just diplomatic stuff. I persisted none the less and eventually he told me what was happening right under our nostril. "The Russians have something going, reports reaching us is that they are working on weapons that we are not sure of and are expanding their territories over to the west. It has been said that there is a Russian plot to sack Luxembourg." That was big, what was Britain's reaction to this news I wandered, and he could tell I was curious, and he quickly responded to my worries: Britain is not going to sit idly by rest assured. We have sent an agent into action, he left early this morning to help us find out the truth behind this and that would help us decide. He shouldn't be too lost though; we have an asset in Russia who'd help make his mission easier".

All this was big news, but my question remained, why did his countenance change yesterday when he wanted to tell me all these. I asked him gently "I know you are worried about these events, but your expression yesterday made me worried, I felt you were in genuine trouble, not that I don't think this is important enough, but you had me worried sir". He smiled and responded quickly "I was worried for you lad; you understand that yeah?" I didn't understand, not in the slightest, I responded him quickly "I don't sir", he continued "let me explain, you were the one assigned to that mission, I knew you weren't ready, you have barely been in England, two years since your last posting and with all that was going with Carla, I couldn't make you go. You needed time to catch your breath".

I had bought you time until something comes up because it will, your line of job but I just felt you needed it, I was touched, the number one citizen of England just protected me, it was something to remember. I left the office, happy and a conflicted. Regardless of how my life was, I would be happy to serve my nation regardless of how long the mission would last, I was giving to stay undercover in Russia as long as ten years, if possible, to ensure the integrity of England remains. I couldn't say however that I wasn't glad about the decision to keep me at home, things were going great with Carla, I enjoyed collaborating closely with the Prime minister.

I walked to my station, sat down with my heart throbbing in my chest with the prospect of being out there once again. It dawned on me at that point that whatever was stalling, I had to fix. I needed to make sure I finished up on all loose ends. It was only just last night I saw Carla, but I left my desk at that minute running down to the coffee shop. She was there yet again, and I demanded another date, I wasn't sure how she'd react, but I didn't care, one thing was in my mind, I had to be with this woman. I wasn't sure when I would be drafted into another mission, but I had to make sure I made her my own. It was a selfish thought however as I didn't consider hers, but I knew she was what I needed to give me a purpose to go out and come back every time.

She was shocked but I knew last night meant lots to her and she agreed to do it again. Date became dates, and even more dates. We started seeing each other and every time she asked about my personal life, I had some fancy story prepared about working in the prime minister's security team, it wasn't a lie necessarily, but it wasn't the complete truth. Dates increased in numbers, we were spending almost every time we weren't at work together, we spent all our free times doing things, seeing places. She had met my family and I hers. Laura and Mark clearly liked me, and I was certain my parents adored her.

We started seeing each other, days became months and after six months of seeing each other, I knew I had to finalise this, I had to make her mine permanently. I was going to propose to Carla, and I was going to marry her as quickly as possible. She clearly doesn't know why I was in a hurry, but I knew I had no control over my life. I didn't know when I'd be taken away and I was too in love with this woman to just leave her alone without reason. It was hard enough not being able to tell her what I do for a living, but I needed her to know I love her whether or not I disappear without a trace very soon.

I planned the time to propose to her, I didn't have friends, just colleagues, my only associates outside of work were my parents and Carla's parents, I had my mom invite them over for dinner and that was where I was going to pop the question. They arrived at exactly 6:30 pm and mark brought a bottle of wine, my dad received it and the pair went into the living room to have whatever conversation they were having, my mom and Laura went into the kitchen to finish dinner preparations. I sat down with Carla on the couch, and we started talking freely like we always do. I was talking towards the direction of living together forever and she was careful to respond.

I feared she was going to refuse my proposal with the way she was responding to my discussion, but I was going to find out none the less. I was going to do it. We were all seated on the table about to have dinner. I shared grace after which we started eating. The focus of the conversation was Carla and me. Both parents wanted to hear all about our relationship, our lives and everything we had to say about ourselves. I let Carla go first and while she talked, she seemed to be enjoying herself, the beauty she boasted radiated over the entire room, like the rays of the sun, her beauty blinded me, but I struggled none the less to behold it, she smiled ever so sweetly as she told her story, I knew it had to be with her.

It was my turn to tell my story, I needed some help from my story to help me get Carla to marry, I started my story, but it wasn't all that chirpy as Carla's. I didn't have much going for me as I couldn't tell them I was a British spy. I stood up at this point still telling my story as Carla's eyes followed me as I left my seat, I walked towards Carla seat still talking, I looked her deep in her eyes and I could see my life in her eyes, I could see both of us in my minds eyes in our old age helping each other cross the street, I held Carla's hands and got to my knees and brought out a small red box, I opened it and in it was a small diamond ring as I said the sweetest words that came to my mind "I clearly don't have the glossiest stories, I've practically not done interesting things and I still don't do interesting things, I wake up in the morning, go to work and get back every day, it's a routine" everyone listened keenly as I talked, she had a gentle smile on her face that made me realise she was receiving my words in good faith. I continued speaking "I'm not easily interested in lots of things, even at school, I wasn't the most involved kid but clearly, I am interested in anything and everything that concerns you. I'm not the smoothest guy definitely so this is tough for me. I don't want to see you at the coffee shop only, I want to see you every day with me, by me. I don't even want you to do anything, I just want you to wake up by me and I will continue from there. Will you marry me?"

She was shocked, the question came out of nowhere but I knew she thought about it in her heart, not that she wasn't eager to say yes and marry me but she was still processing the question in her head, I could see tears roll down her cheek as both parents kept pushing her to say yes, she eventually said yes and I got up from my kneeling position and she hugged me as tightly as possible. My worries about her refusing had gone away, I was the happiest man around, I had the woman of my dreams right next to me and she was going to stay there.

My father for joy went into the artic of the building and brought out one of his stored wines, as a kid, I always thought my father valued his wines more than he did he and my mother, his wine cellar was out of both our reaches. I always wondered why he had so many wines and never drank them, the concept of collecting didn't make sense to me. He brought out a bottle of wine and with pride he said with a fake Spanish accent "this my family is a bottle of the 1950 Ruffino croce d'oro 'salento' Bianco vino liquoroso, Puglia Italy.

It's a rare white blend" we all laughed as we knew even, he didn't know what that meant. He got most of these wines from his father who like him was a wine enthusiast and collector. It made sense, the entire night but amidst the festivities, the rare white blend wine, the rose flowers beautifully laden across the dinner table, the most beautiful sight to behold was Carla, my wife. It felt good to call her that in my head, it would feel even better to say it to her in person.

CHAPTER EIGHTEEN: TURNING POINT

It had been over five years since my return from Saudi Arabia and two years since I married the love of my life, Carla. The tension brewing in Eastern Europe like the Prime minister mentioned to me had long been forgotten by me. I clearly wasn't keeping track of the undercover mission as only very few people were supposed to know such mission even existed and that was the prime minister, the secretary of defence, the permanent secretary in charge of the GCHQ and the directors of the MI5 and MI6. It was that classified. Regardless of what his mission was, he seemed to be doing alright because if he wasn't, the alarm would have gone up. There would have been measures made to ensure Britain doesn't get the stick for what was going on in independent Russia.

I had forgotten it because life was going fine for me, I had told Carla so many times that I was a just a guard in the prime minister's security detail that I was starting to believe it myself. I had been so out of commission from active work that I was beginning to think I was just a family-oriented person. I had showed up one morning when I was informed by the prime minister about a supposed meeting between himself, the secretary of defence, the permanent secretary in charge of GCHQ and the directors of both MI5 and MI6, I knew that there was trouble.

The meeting was to hold at Downing Street. It started at about 8:00 am in the morning and I waited outside for deliberations to end. It lasted a very long time, at about 10:00am, I was still waiting for them to conclude discussions. Whatever was going on I said to myself has to be something very important to keep men this busy locked inside this long. It had something to do with British intelligence or national security.

When the meeting was finally over and all parties had left, the Prime minister summoned me into his office for a conversation, he offered me a glass of fine whisky which I obliged. He wasn't saying anything in particular but spent time just talking about the little things In life "when you think you have it all under control, life brings you to realize that you don't, that you are just a player in some grand scheme that is not of your making nor can be controlled by you", silence filled the air, I didn't understand what he was talking about and replying was almost impossible, I didn't want to say anything that would make me look or sound insensitive, I waited for him to continue talking so I can pick up on whatever it was he was talking about, he continued "we were a step closer a while ago but right now, we are acres behind". At this rate, I didn't know what he was talking about, but I could sense his concern and worry over something, I needed to say something to calm him down but as I was about to say anything, his secretary rushed in the office asking him to get the phone that there was something he should hear.

He picked the phone, it was the secretary of defence, whatever was said to him, I didn't know but instantly, he jumped off of his table that he was sitting on, headed for the door and told me we weren't done with this conversation "there's something really important I have to talk to you about, I might not be back before you leave but this is something we are going to have to talk about as soon as you show up in the morning", he rushed out of the office. I was still there confused about what just happened or what was actually happening when the secretary came and ushered me out of the office.

Work was slow for the rest of the day, I did close to nothing at the prime minister's office, the only thing I did was talk to him about political issues, I wasn't an agent, I was more like an aide or adviser or something, it wasn't what I signed up for and I loved my country but it offered some sort of stability in my life running around the world spying was fun and stuff but at the moment, I was pretty comfortable with what I had.

Whenever I felt conflicted, I usually just went to Carla's coffee shop, she was the only person in the world that knew how to clear my head, she didn't even need to say or do anything, just by looking at her alone, I was able to find inner peace. I left Downing Street, headed straight for Carla's coffee shop, it was a twenty minutes' walk from where I walked so, I opted to walk there, as I walked, the beauty of London became obvious to me. For the first time in my life, I saw the rich history and culture in the buildings in London, I appreciated the town for what it was, I thought about the countless numbers of people that would want to do Russia harm as a statement or whatever. I thought to myself that it could be as a result of one of these threats that the prime minister was not feeling comfortable. Something must have been wrong because I had never seen him this tense since I met the man, I mean the man knew how to keep his cool like a seasoned professional. He could pass for a spy in British intelligence for his ability to keep his cool but right now that cool had gone out the window. I could help, I knew it and I was willing to.

I got to Carla's coffee shop and I met her at the door leaving just as I was approaching, I called out to her and she stopped, looking at me with a smile on her face, a face that had looked as beautiful to me as it did the day I met her, we had been married two years now but it still felt to me like two days. I ran up to her and hugged her, she liked it but she knew something was off and she had to ask being the missus and all. "What's wrong Dave?" I looked at the floor, this woman could read me better than she could read a book, and I tried to brush the question to the side "it's just work stuff, nothing to worry about", she nodded her head, she wasn't convinced it was nothing to worry about but despite how much she persisted, I kept on saying it was nothing, I killed off the argument when I asked "can't a man just come around to see his loving wife? Do I need to have a problem to come here to see you?" she smiled and said 'no, just that you seemed pretty worried when you approached me" "I am fine" I cut in. "you don't have to worry about me". She laughed it off as she said "that is basically my only job, worrying about you, not doing that would mean failing at the only job I have". We both laughed as I chipped in yet again "what about the coffee shop? Isn't that a job?" "It's a side business, the main job is worrying and taking care of my baby".

Like magic, I was feeling better, I had forgotten for a moment the troubles in the heart of the prime minister. The last time he had similar countenance, it was to tell me that Russia was expanding and that an agent had been sent to do recon and come back with information necessary for actions to be taken. Maybe that is where the problem lies, what if the agent had been compromised, and just like that I was back where I was running from. I held Carla close, I was going to live in the moment, I was going to talk to my wife, I am going to keep falling in love with her over and over throughout the time we spent here together, I wasn't going to bother too much about what was going on at work at least not now. For now Carla was it for me. I knew however that I couldn't avoid it forever, in the morning, I'd be returned to the harsh realization that there was a national issue and as an intelligence agent, I had to be worried.

CHAPTER NINETEEN: PREPARATION

I got to work as early the next day, I headed for the prime minister's office but I was refused access because he was in an important meeting, I had to wait outside for him to finish for me to go in and discuss whatever it was that left him distraught the day before. I had waited a while a while and was about to leave when the secretary told me that I was wanted in the meeting. Me? Wanted in a meeting with the prime minister? Of course, I entered his office a lot of times but those were impromptu visits, they weren't meetings with other people.

I hesitated but clearly it wasn't going away so I went into the office where I met alongside the prime minister, the secretary of defence and the permanent secretary in charge of the Government Communications Headquarters (GCHQ). What were my superiors doing here at Downing and why they in a closed door meeting with the prime minister and most importantly, why were they looking at me like there was someone or something standing behind me that I wasn't aware of? I walked into the office, I saluted them all and I was eased. Silence fell over the room, I knew there was something I was going to be told now that would be really big, I don't know what it was, but I was an agent and I was ready for it.

The prime minister offered me a seat and I accepted, I sat down, and all three men fixed their gaze on me. This was clearly a mission briefing but I didn't know where I was going to next. I waited in anticipation for one of them to say a word, but it seemed they wanted it down on me, the importance of the situation, hence everyone stayed quiet. I clearly couldn't speak unless spoken to so I waited patiently. It was the prime minister who spoke first. "I have known you a long time since we met at Saudi and I must say you have been an important addition to the British secret service, which was why you were the first person that came to mind when this mission was brought up". I accepted the compliments and all that but what was this mission that I was chosen for. I wanted to hear about it so bad. I needed to know what it was about.

He continued, this time with the exact mission briefing. I listened keenly, not to miss any information from what he was saying, he went on "this is really big for everybody involved, for you, for me, for the entire UK and even some smaller countries in Europe. Reports reached us at some points last year that Russia were working on some weapons, chemical weapons and that they were proposing taking over some smaller European nations, they are trying to expand their reach, we acted on that information and send an agent undercover to sort out the details of the information and report back to us. He was doing a splendid job on site but recently, after informing us that he was very close to something major, he went off grid. All efforts to contact the asset had proved abortive. We suspect he has been taken into custody. That being the case, he as an agent knows that upon being compromised, he is on his own but our fears were brought back again when we discovered the Russian government were working on torture project, one they called project x. this is classified information from another spy on the ground. It is on record that everybody on whom project x had been used on couldn't hold back whatever information they had. We don't know yet if project x is induced or it's just a torture apparatus but we don't want to take any chances. We are almost sure he hadn't been captured because if he has, they'd have used x on him and he'd have spilled and the backlash would have started but that the Russians are still quiet means that they haven't found out about him". I was interested in the information but listened keenly. He continued "your mission is simple, find him or what's left of him or get whatever information you can about him and send it back home but if you can't find him, find out what the bollocks is going on in Russia and send us something, anything".

He was done talking and I could ask questions now and I did "who is this agent I am looking for and where exactly in Russia is he at the moment?" "All those information would be given to you when you are ready" I nodded my head as I stood up to make my exit from the room. I saluted once again as I walked out of the room. I had a lot to achieve. I didn't know if I could go through with this mission. It was nothing like Saudi Arabia, I didn't have a small army, I didn't have people who would spur me on and even help me in this mission alone, I was going behind enemy lines on my own and I had to account for not just myself but another agent. This was clearly bigger than Saudi Arabia but I knew that my time in the Middle East had prepared me for what I was going to be facing now and it was nothing I couldn't handle.

Moments later, I sat down at my station, thinking about what I had to do, how I was going to infiltrate the Russians to sneak out an agent. The worries on my mind, gave me a hard time focusing on the days duty in front of me, this was a big ask but I had to do it none the less. I rested my back on the chair and placed my legs on the desk in front of me, my thoughts wandered far into the very embers of possibilities, my death in Russia. It was not a possibility that was impossible. I had come face to face with death and I had escaped a couple of times, maybe this time, the grim reaper would have his way and place his cold hands of death over my shoulders and take me with him to his hallows where he drops men like me.

I thought of it all, another English spy caught in Russian space would suggest that the UK was behind all of it so if I was going to die at all, had to die away from Russian eyes, to keep the integrity of my nation uncompromised. That was most important to me than my own life. As my thoughts ran through the isle of negativity, there was only one positive amidst them, that was Carla, I had just met the girl of my dreams and just like that, there was a chance I wasn't going to see her again. The mission didn't seem like it gives me any chance to sort out my issues before I left but one thing was certain, I had to say goodbye to Carla before I left but she could never know where I was going to. I left the office earlier than usual. I hadn't been briefed on departure, so I thought I had a little time to say goodbye.

Carla met me at the door of the coffee shop, she was living for the day and I was in a hurry to meet her before she left, I had studied her so well, I knew when she closed and when she opened, I wasn't obsessed but she meant that much to me. I knew at that point that I had to spend what was left with my wife. She looked at me I had an expression yet again they suggested that something was wrong. I couldn't say for sure what it was but she could see that clearly something was off.

I looked at Carla with so much sadness, I wanted to tell her all that was going on but I knew I couldn't, it was part of the arrangement I had made when I joined the agency. She didn't have to go through this with me after all I didn't tell her what I did for a living. I clinched my fist ground my teeth and I walked towards her, I hugged her tightly as tears rolled down my cheeks.

Carla was shocked, she didn't know how to respond to what I was saying but she hugged me back anyways. She had a way of making my troubles go away and I wouldn't trade that for anything. Time flies when you're having fun they say and just like that I had spent the last five minutes just hugging Carla. She knew something was off but like all my other issues, she was sure I couldn't say. She knew if she asked, I'd just brush it off with my usual excuse, work stuff.

"What's wrong Dave?" She asked as she freed herself from my hugs and held my face gently, the setting sun reflected in her eyes as I beheld the beauty of her glowing skin. I didn't know how to say this anymore gently, I had to just say it anyhow. "I'm going away for a while. I don't know how long I'll be away but I have to". With a smile on her face, she let go of my face, she was sad clearly, but she was trying to be strong for the both of us as she could tell I wasn't being strong enough.

"When do you leave?" She asked, I didn't even have the answer to that, I just responded anyway I could "I don't even know yet, I haven't been told. Rest assured, I'll try and be back as soon as I can". She knew I was just saying that to console her somewhat. She smiled and said "at least you are still around, let's go home and have dinner".

Dinner was quiet, I couldn't say the reason why I was leaving town so soon and Carla wasn't going to ask, she was always okay knowing I had a life of my own that I didn't have to involve her in, it clearly wasn't easy for her but she knew that if we were going to live together in peace for the rest of our lives, she had to accept it. I was putting her through discomfort so early in our marriage.

Should I tell her? Definitely I couldn't, tell her, doing that would put her life and that of her parents in danger. I had to face my problems myself. After eating the quietest meals of our lives, I was doing the dishes when she walked into the kitchen, hugged me from behind "I reckon you'd come back to me eventually, yeah?" She was clearly in pains. It was a recon and an extraction mission, and a more experienced agent has supposedly been captured or killed in the line of duty. Returning alive wasn't something I could promise my darling wife but telling her I wouldn't destroy her.

I was the man, it was my job to take care of her and I knew I had to give her an assurance no matter how small "I will come back to you. We promised to live the rest of our lives together and no matter how hard you chase me away, I will always be here under your skin nagging the shit out of you".

For the first time since I told her I was going, she smiled a little, I loved seeing her smile and I cherished that little smile she just gave me. We finished doing the dishes together, went to the couch and listened to 50s music on the recorder. In no time she was asleep and she held on to me as tightly as a new born its mother. Clearly she didn't want me to leave her side but it was something I had to do.

The night was long and for someone who had someone on his bed, it was lonely. I thought about possibilities in Russia. What would I face? Would I find the agent? Why did he go off grid? Too many questions to answer but I clearly couldn't find the answers in London. I had to be in Russia. Yet again my life was going to be on the line for my nation, but I wouldn't have it any other way.

We both slept off on the couch, Carla not willing to let me go even for a second and me very much comfortable with her warm embrace, I held her back tightly as I fell asleep to the sound of beautiful music and the breath of the woman, I love coming down my chest. It was the kind of nights I wish I could put on repeat.

CHAPTER TWENTY: ALL TOO WELL

I was up as early as I could, I sat down on the couch at home trying to bring myself to accept going away from my wife. The night before I woke up completely seemed very long but just when it was time for me to ponder some more about life, time was racing like it was aiming for a finished line.

I was up and I set Carla properly on the couch so she could sleep without any pains, I went to the bathroom to set myself for work. I knew in my heart that any day from my now I would have to leave. It didn't occur to me how sudden it would be. I stood in front of the mirror, looking at myself, giving myself the much needed confidence boost. I did need it. I didn't know what to expect this time, I hoped it didn't have to involve as much casualties as Saudi Arabia but then again, unlike Saudi Arabia, not many agents was involved in this. If lives were going to be taken, it's going to be mine or the agent who was already on ground.

As I stood in the bathroom, having a meeting with the different emotions and thoughts that formed my person at the time, I heard the door open as Carla walked in. "Is it the time yet?" She asked, I shook my head to suggest not yet but it wasn't enough to brighten her face. She couldn't bring out that smile I loved so much. I held her close to me with her head on my chest, I could feel my heart throb and I needed her to feel it too. I needed her to know that I wasn't leaving because I wanted to, I was leaving because I had to. She held me closely for a while until I freed myself. I had to leave now. I planted a gentle kiss on her head as I left the bathroom to ready myself for work.

I was set in next to no time and I walked up to her making breakfast, I sat down to have whatever she was making but the phone rang almost as immediately as I sat down. It was a call from GCHQ, I wasn't going to report at Downing Street today, I was to report at GCHQ in Cheltenham. That was where I'd get my final briefing and when I'd know when exactly I was leaving for Russia.

I had to leave even before having breakfast, Carla didn't like the idea of me going away for a while but I had to, I hugged her yet again, I stayed that way for almost 30seconds and when I freed myself, I kissed her on the forehead, I told her "it'll be okay, I'll be fine and you will as well. We both will be fine" and I left the house.

It would take me a longer time to get to Cheltenham than it would to Downing so I knew I had to spend less time at home. I headed for the subway as it would be the quickest route to get to HQ. As I tried to get through the queue to board the train, I saw English men, women and children going about their day to day lives in regular fashion, this was what I signed up to protect. Even if my wife is heartbroken that I have to live, I'm sure she'd be super proud of me if she knew what I did for a living. I don't know if she'd love me more but she'd be proud of me. I had always felt we should be able to tell our loved ones about what we do as it was nothing to hide but it was for the best that we don't.

I arrived Cheltenham in time, it had been a while I had been at HQ, it felt different as I saw workers troop in and out of the ever busy building, there was a reason the building was called the doughnut and one would wonder, for an agency who prides in her secret operations, the building was really noticeable. It earned its name from an actual doughnut, it was designed like a doughnut and covered a significant portion of land. Its lobby always had at least two hundred people. It was good to be among my fellows once again but I didn't miss the relative peace I got at Downing Street.

I remember when I signed up at GCHQ, I signed up and I was drafted into the composite signals organization (CSO) which existed for information gathering and analysis. I had a degree in Finance, and I could gather financial information and analyse them through which decisions could be made. I never knew that that would take me out to Saudi Arabia for my first mission, now being drafted again for a recon and extraction mission, it was not the first order of business for me but it was business none the less.

I walked into the lobby where I met a woman on the desk, it was early, but the doughnut was already packed. I introduced myself as David Scarlet and she responded like she had been waiting for me. She gave me directions to where I was supposed to have my meeting. It was the top floor, the fourth floor of the HQ. It was a sort of executive floor for the top brass of British intelligence. I felt really good about being there for the first time in my career, it explained to me just how important whatever my mission was and just how serious I had to take it.

I made way to the top floor, I couldn't keep them waiting, the lady I just met made it look they've been waiting for me. I rushed into the relay controlled elevator, not as effective as the 21st century ones but did the job none the less. In no time, I was in the fourth floor. I rushed over to the office she told me, it had on the door, Director Mrs Rosa McGomery. I knocked and I was ushered in. I met a woman and two men and from past knowledge, they were the Directors of MI5 and MI6. I saluted as they offered me a seat. I sat down, I had already received a mission briefing so this was definitely just a closing up for me to go with as I headed into Russia.

Mrs Rosa looked at me and with so much passion as she started to speak, I could tell she wanted the issue sorted out as quickly as possible. She was a firm woman in her 50s, short brown hair and brown eyes, she wasn't the tallest, but she looked like she had a lot of control in her. Her voice was firm, it had power. When she spoke, I was compelled to listen, she was like the siren in Greek mythology, but she pushed people to action, not with the beauty of her voice but the power of control in it. I negated all thoughts as I listened to her with rapt attention.

"I know you already have an idea of what you are going to Russia to do, it seems a simple smash and grab, you break in grab the agent and live, but I want to assure you beforehand that it won't be that easy. There is a long standing rivalry between the British and the Russians and trust me, they'd be on the lookout for guys like you. What I'm trying to say is this, stay low and out of sight, find the agent and get out. You know that should you get caught, the British government has no business with you and you should never give out state secrets". I responded positively to all she said but she wasn't done talking, she continued "you are going to drop off at Tver, a small town 110 miles northwest of Moscow. We have an asset on ground, she has information that might prove useful about the whereabouts of the agent on ground, rendezvous in Tver, and pick up what is necessary and go about your mission". She paused, picked up a glass of water and gulped it down her throat in a hurry, she must have been really dehydrated I thought.

I wanted to ask questions, but she clearly wasn't done speaking so I waited for her to finish what she started "a lot is going on Russia that we are not aware of, we need you to go in and out knowing fully well that the fate of the United Kingdom rests on your shoulders. It's a bit much to put on you but you were recommended for this job. I didn't think you have the skill set for this but for whatever reason, the prime minister trusted you and demanded that you take this mission. You best be making that old geezer proud. Any questions?" She had finally stopped talking and I could ask my questions. She seemed a no nonsense woman clearly, I had to make my questions as smart as I could not to let off even an ounce of inexperience, she already doesn't think I'm good enough for the mission anyways.

I stuttered as I asked my questions. My questions were simple "do we know exactly what happened to the agent on ground, has he been captured or did he fall off grid on his own choice? " I needed to know if I was going to burst him out of some huge Russian jail or I was just going to find a man who had lost his fighting spirit. The difficulty of the mission defined how I was going to approach it, one of the men in the room was the one who responded to my question "he was my agent from MI6, he was doing just fine, sending us information through our asset for a while and all of a sudden he just stopped. Project x is already being used, we believe that if he had been captured, project x should have been used on him and the asset would have been compromised but the asset has managed to remain in contact so there is the likelihood that he hasn't been captured, that is for you to find out when you get there". The response was direct and did justice to my question, but it opened the situation up for further questions and I grabbed it by the balls, "this asset you speak of, can he be trusted completely?" The man replied quickly "yes, why?" I explained at once," it could be that the agent has been compromised and the asset is just playing along to drive the UK to a corner".

The lady nodded her head before she responded "I get your point mate, but we could all be compromised, we never know. As agents, we trust no one, we receive our mission briefing and go out there risking our lives trusting no one. The asset might be compromised, we never know but for now, we want to believe he hasn't. He's the only eyes we have on site. You need him not to be compromised because if he is then you are much fucked". She was very right in every sense of the word fucked but I needed to know that the man I was placing my life in his hands was someone I could trust.

I needed information however of the agent I was supposed to be meeting and a file was handed over to me, it had all I needed to know about who I was looking for. As I opened the file to access the information, I heard the questions "do you accept the mission?" I hesitated about five seconds and I said "Yes ma, I do". She continued "very well agent, you leave in two days, your flight leaves the London city airport. You are an art enthusiast, a successful business man by name Jimmy Clayton and you are going to be at the Tverskaya Oblastnaya Kartinnaya Galereya, in search of the most famous Russian painting, Valentin Serov's "Portrait of Maria Tsetlin".

She continued after giving me time to assimilate "that's your identity, you know what to do with the information, your flight drops off at Moscow Sheremetyevo, we will contact the and fix a meet up for the both of you the day after you land, you will lodge at hotel Tver and the both of you can arrange your exchange. It is important to note however that the only people who know you are British intelligence are the people in this room this very instant and the prime minister and the plan is to keep it that way. So stay safe mate and God speed".

I got up from the chair I had been sitting throughout the briefing, I saluted the officers as I left. I held tightly the file I had been given, it didn't have much in it, just the identity of the agent and nothing more. I didn't know where exactly in Tver in Russia he was, I didn't even know where. Tver was in Russia, heck I had never been to Russia before but I guess there was a first time for everything, but I wished it wouldn't have been under these circumstances. I had a lot to learn, I didn't know the first thing about arts, I had a lot to study if I was going to fool anyone that I was an art enthusiast and I had just two days to do that. The art gallery I was supposedly visiting will be having an auction in a short while as Mrs Rosa mentioned just off her breath while she briefed, I figured that would be the best rendezvous point with the asset, he'd probably have what I needed in a file and I'd receive it quietly there, he didn't have to be involved, just drop it off with me somehow, I pick it up and I'll be off on my own.

I hoped that for the sake of England, everyone was clean and that the agent on sight hadn't been captured. I had always wished that my missions wouldn't be met with violence of any kind and every time I did that, I was met with resistance, I didn't know if this time, I should wish for resistance just so I wouldn't get resistance, but I was sure that wasn't how it worked. I left the office with mixed feelings as I headed for the elevator. I was both scared and confident. I knew it was a mission to save my country but I was going to be behind enemy lines without backup, I wasn't going as a diplomat this time, I was going with a pretend identity, it was nothing like Saudi Arabia, this was it, people wouldn't clap at me for being a diplomat in Russia, I was a spy and I was sure there'd be some sort of reward for any Russian that kills a foreign spy.

CHAPTER TWENTY ONE: CONTACT

I was back at the elevator, it was supposed to be less than five minutes to get back to the lobby, but those five minutes seemed like forever, I wanted to keep looking and analysing the file I was given, of course it wasn't finance related as that what was I knew how to do but I had to look at the file critically. I got to the lobby in a short time and as I headed for the door, the chills of uncertainty ran through my spine, it was happening all over again, I had a big mission before me. I didn't stop for a second to look back at the amazing structure that was the doughnut, I couldn't tell if that was the last time I'd see it or not but I wasn't going to look back. It had to be forward ever for me from now on. I headed for the train station, I knew the next few weeks and months were going to be important and tense, they were going to be figuring out factors for what happened next for me. I had to get home as quickly as possible, find out what I could about art or something. I argued why I couldn't have been a financial person of some sort in Tver, why art. I knew nothing of the topic, I thought to myself, but I figured it was because of the gallery that was opening in a little over three days. They must have put a lot of thought into all this to get me going with so much detail. They had done their part, it was time to do mine.

I needed to go to Carla at the coffee shop as I was in one of those moods where she alone could fix me up but I knew I had a short time to go from being a family man with knowledge in finance to become an art enthusiast and a business man so I opted to go home and do a little bit of research. I was sure the only artist I knew at the time was

Pablo Picasso and Leonardo Da Vinci. I needed that research a lot more than I thought. I got home in time enough to study for some hours before Carla would return. It wasn't the most enjoyable experience, but it was absolutely necessary. Tver, I thought to myself, I will be neck deep in enemy territory, I needed to avoid any slip up, the fear of being compromised and captured was all the motivation I needed to become Jimmy Clayton, a businessperson and an art enthusiast. I knew exactly when Carla would be home and I made sure to have done what I could and clear the entire place. I didn't want to explain too much to Carla. I had to make her a little bit happy before I left in two days.

Carla returned home just about the time she usually does and by then, I had tidied everywhere. When she walked into the door, I rushed over to her, hugged her, kissed her, I even carried her up for a few seconds. Carla was confused, for all she knew, when we both left in the morning, we were sad. What had changed? I'm sure she thought in her heart that I wasn't going away anymore but she had to confirm "what are we celebrating?" she asked, I answered quickly "does a man need an occasion to hug and kiss his wife?" she smiled in her response "you know that's not what I meant", I dropped her, she thought that was it, but I held her on to her waist as I pulled her towards me, I kissed her and the kiss wasn't so gentle, she responded in the same energy. The kissing continued for a while as we made way for the room. The sex that followed was ecstatic, it was amazing. I thought to myself "maybe I have to go a lot more if it'd make the sex this amazing". It lasted for a while and after we were both drained of energy, we laid down on the bed and it was time to break the details of my leaving to her.

I spoke in a hushed tune, I had taken her out of this world, and I had to bring her back as gently as I could, "I now have more information about my leaving", she was shocked back to reality "I thought all that celebration was because you didn't have to go anymore?" I tried to fake a smile, but it wasn't forthcoming "of course I still have to go but this time, the story is clear". The joy she had was gone again, we were back to where we were when we left in the morning "ok, go on with it, tell me what you have to say". I could feel a little hostility in her voice, she was sad again but I knew I was doing the right thing, so I continued "I am going to Portugal with some top government official", "to do what?" she asked. I was shocked she asked me that "of course I didn't know that my job is just to ensure they make it to and fro, simple".

I could not tell her the truth and the fake information I just gave her calmed her down a little, I could feel her comfort knowing it wasn't anything wrong illegal or bad that was taking me out of town. I was hoping she didn't ask me when I was to return but I was brought back to earth when she asked the question "when do you leave and when do you return?" the two questions I dreaded, she was asking them both at one go. The answers I had for her on these questions would definitely leave her heartbroken but not telling her would make it worse, so I had to. "I leave on Sunday at the London airport, and I don't know when I will be back, that decision is left for the diplomats I was going with". Almost as immediately as I gave that answer, she turned her back and said good night, I could hear as she cried, she tried to make it as quiet as possible but she couldn't. I got very close to her and held her tightly as we both slept off eventually.

Saturday went by fast, it wasn't my best day as the house was as quiet as a library located in a cemetery. Carla barely talked to me and when it was about 6pm, she told me she was going to my parents place. I knew if she did that, mom would constantly keep calling, I tried to convince her with a nice dinner for two but she wouldn't have it. She walked up to me, kissed my forehead and told me "they are going to be my best friends for as long as you'll be away, I know it would be impossible to reach you while you are there but maybe if I slept in your old room, I won't miss you so much". I get she had to be close to my parents somehow but what about sleeping in the room in which we have memories, our own room. I blamed it on just not wanting to be alone so I accepted. I opted to drive her over, but she refused suggesting she'd drive herself and I agreed. She left shortly after and I had enough time to ponder my actions, my plans, the mission, how to be stealthy enough to go in and out of Russia without being noticed.

It was back to the couch again for me, I felt the couch was my own place where I had my best thoughts or where I wallow better. I had a bottle of beer on my hand, I could barely drink it, we were headed into the embers of the day and my thoughts was still as active as it was when I was most awake. I laid there with my thoughts as I tries to discern the best cause of action, while I was deep in thoughts, the phone rang, I picked it up and it was Carla. She was hoping she could talk me out of going somehow but she gave up when she noticed I wasn't giving in to her demands, she stopped and wished me success. She made a statement that made me reconsider the entire mission, but I couldn't refuse it anymore, I had already accepted and I wasn't a deserter. As we talked on the phone, she said "I reckon I can't talk you out of this decision so I have to support you, I love you loads and I hope and pray that you come back soon, I'm really going to miss you, me and Junior and your parents and all". It was like my brain was on delay, it hadn't processed the information quickly, I was about appreciating her kindness when I realized I heard Junior, I stopped to respond and she continued "you heard me right, I'm pregnant, I did not want to say it at home so it doesn't look like I was trying to guilt trip you into staying but it doesn't go without saying, I'd love it if you stayed but I know you are only trying to provide us with the best life that life has to offer and I appreciate you for that. I love you". I was about to respond when she dropped the call, I called a hundred times but she wouldn't pick. I thought about driving over to my parent's, but she had already taken the car. It was already 1:00am and I didn't think I could make it so I just managed to force myself to sleep.

I couldn't sleep for very long, I was going to be a father, just about the same time as I was going on a mission that I couldn't guarantee my life. I was up as early as 5am contemplating whether to go see my wife at my parent's or just wait until I was back. I needed clarification and details. I was going to be a father, of course I was excited but now the mission just got a lot harder. I decided to go to Carla but just as I picked my jacket and my luggage, the phone rang,

I rushed to it thinking it was Carla but when I answered, it was the Director of GCHQ, my ETA was 6:00 am. I wouldn't make it to my parents and back to the airport in that time so I had to leave without Carla. I left a note on the table which says "at the time you needed me the most, I couldn't be there. It doesn't say anything about how much I love you. I left because I had to, I'll be back and I'd love you both to the end of time". I locked the door as I left my home.

It was a cold morning, the drive to the airport was lonely, and it felt to me like I had given up everything that loved me. My heart ached heavily and I could hear my heart beat in my ears, the rhythm wasn't normal as I felt like my heart couldn't hold the pain. I squeezed unto the coat I had in my hand trying to somehow believe I could hold unto Carla that closely once again. I tried to take my mind away from it but it was to no avail, I wasn't thinking about Tver, but about my wife and kid. Before long, I was at the London airport and there was a man dressed in black suit who sat down by me as I waited clearance to board the flight. He left a package on the seat without saying a word as he got up and left just before it was my turn to be dealt with. I figured he was an agent and the file was for me. I picked it up as I walked to be cleared for flying.

I wandered what was contained within but I had to wait till I was airborne to confirm. I flew first class as I was already in character from the airport. I opened the file and it was a full information on the agent I was going to recover. His names was Harold pike, he was an agent with MI6, he had a much decorated career but just like that, he probably might have been killed. That was the life of an agent, it didn't matter, as long as you were serving your nation but whenever something happens, you are immediately replaced. I couldn't tell why I liked the job so much but I did. The flight wasn't the longest, in about 4 hours, we were already at the Moscow Sheremetyevo airport. They had ready a convoy on ground that would receive me and accompany me to Hotel Tver where I would be staying.

The drive from the airport to the hotel didn't take long, I took time to take in the beauty of the small city. It had a rich Russian heritage. The waters teamed with beautiful architecture to display a city so beautiful that hosted tourists from all over the globe. It was a perfect blend of natural and artificial, the trees, the hills sat perfectly behind and around the works of arts that were built by men's hands. It was however the perfect place to hide any research facility, and no one would find out. What better place to hide your loot than right under the nose of authority? They'd never find out. The Russians can leave their biggest asset right here in Tver and nobody would bother to check. It looked a city Carla would love to visit, she always said she wanted to travel the world someday. In a short while, I was at the hotel Tver. It was a spectacle, the hotel. The hotel was located just at the outskirts of town, it covered a large plot of land, and the view was amazing. I felt for a second that I was on a vacation, but I knew I had to keep my heads up. I couldn't afford any slip ups if I was going to finish this mission and leave Russia as quickly as possible. I checked into the room. It had finally started, my second big mission. I was In Tver already and I was more determined to achieve success now more than ever.

CHAPTER TWENTY TWO: PAINT PAINTS PAINTING

I arrived Tver on Sunday and I checked into the hotel Tver but the only thing on my mind was the art gallery and a way to find the asset, I was looking forward to rounding up and leaving Tver as soon as possible. I didn't want to contact him over phone as that might prove costly. I tried to remain calm, if I couldn't meet him at the art gallery, I would extend my stay by a while to ensure I meet him eventually.

My first night at Tver, there was peaceful, I laid down on the king size bed in the suite. I was getting treatment worthy of an agent after all. For all we go through, we deserved treatments of this nature occasionally. I was still conflicted within myself. On one side, allegiance to duty and on the other, love for my pregnant wife. I had already made a choice hence I was in Tver but it didn't mean I didn't love my wife any less.

I laid down on the bed thinking about a lot of things until I fell asleep. The night was long and peaceful, as I drifted into dream land, I left my worries behind. It was like my subconscious understood that in a short time, I'll be faced with problems that I might not be able to handle hence it gave me that night off from all the worrying. I slept like a newborn who had been fed very well.

It was a day again, the art auction was scheduled for 7:00pm, I was going to be there by 6:30 pm tops, I had to blend in, I was an art enthusiast but the usual art enthusiast wouldn't know who I was as they probably have never heard or seen me in one of these art auctions, I was going to do a tough job convincing them that I had been doing this for a while. I had my last preparation for a long night. It was the supposed night to meet the asset. It was a big night for me and it had to be perfect, I wasn't here for a vacation after all. The day was slow, I was afraid visibly but the past few days had been leading to this point. It was now or never. I had to put up a show and wow the audience. I went through my art lessons one more time and I looked ready. I just had to be calm and everything will be fine. I laid down on the bed and fell asleep. My mind in my sleep went to his place of peace, it went to Carla, my beloved wife. I knew that's where I wanted to be, right there with Carla attending to all her pregnancy demands but right here is where I ought to be. I slept off and had no dreams. I woke up thirty minutes to the auction, I got dressed and informed the hotel for the chauffeur to pick me up.

***

I arrived in a GAZ 69, a pure Russian beast of a vehicle adapted from war vehicles used during World War 2, I felt like royalty as I boarded the vehicle. The Tverskaya Oblastnaya Kartinnaya Galereya was in the middle of town and the Hotel Tver was on the outskirts, so it took a while for me to get there. By the time I did, there was a small gathering of elites already there, it was a red-carpet event. It was an event indeed. There were cameras and pictures, I tried my hardest to avoid the cameras, I didn't want to be seen in any pictures. That would be a big blow on my mission.

I tried my hardest to avoid any form of publicity and I headed straight for the gallery itself boycotting the red carpet and the paparazzi. The paintings were indeed dazzling, but I walked straight for Valentin Serov's portrait of Maria Tsetlin. I looked at it and it was detailed to the very last detail. "Beautiful, isn't it?" I turned around to find a beautiful woman standing beside me, she continued "it was drawn in 1910 by Valentin servo. I read Maria Tsetlin was a woman of substance and had to be remembered somehow, the artist decided to draw this and keep it as a memory of her". I liked her courage to talk to an absolute stranger and I wanted to keep the conversation going "I see you know your art, I do know a thing or two about art myself. I have been looking for this painting to add to my collection." she smiled "pardon my manner, the name's Daria Iyanov" "and I'm Jimmy Clayton" I responded as I stretched my hand for her and she gave me her right hand which I kissed gently before letting go.

"Quite the gentleman, aren't we?" she sounded like she had lived all her live in England, she spoke with an English accent, but she had Russian names. I pushed it to the side but she was determined to have more conversations with me. "I particularly I'm not a fan of the Maria Tsetlin, I won't lie to you, it speaks volumes, the power of feminine determination and all that. I like her focus but I'm one of those girls who accept that it's a man's world", she knew her art "I am interested in the fine details of the painting, the motif behind painting it isn't the target, I like his paint strokes every now and then, it is so detailed you could see the crease on her clothing. I might say also that I'm pulled in by the finesse with which he graced her beauty. I'm not bothered by who she is but I get a hard on for good painting". She smiled at my perspective. "I have been chasing arts a while, I haven't seen you before", she replied "do you just fancy

Russian arts or you go after any arts?" That was a direct question, I had to talk my way out of it "I'm a businessman, I don't always do the pursuit myself, I just decided I needed time off, hence I came all the way for this one and I must say, it's quite delightful".

"It's always a beauty, Tver this time of year, no wonder it's always packed with tourists from all over the world". I cut in. "a true spectacle it is, a wonder of a city" she responded. I haven't been here long but I must say, I've loved every moment I've been in Tver" I said as I admired the grace with which she carried herself. We moved on from the Maria Tsetlin painting to other paintings. We had a decent conversation until she said she had to leave. She hugged me, kissed me on the cheek and told me "I'd love to meet you again another time probably in a different setting from this one", "I'd like that" I said to her as she walked away.

The rest of the night was quiet and uneventful, had some conversations here and others there but none like the one with Daria Iyanov. She was stuck in my thoughts. Her long flowing red dress, her hair gently curled just in front of her eyes. It was like the hair was there to protect men like me from looking into her eyes. Her big brown eyes were like Meduza's gaze capable of turning ones heart solid to the beauty of other women but pulling you closer to her and her red painted lips that made her eyes even more beautiful. The perfectly placed curves on her body and her fair skin that would make models quiver. She was art herself, one I would pay a lot more for than those paintings on the wall. When she left, I tried at that time, to find the asset but nobody seemed like one, I started to think it was a waste of time coming here, the asset was a no show and I had to go back to the hotel with nothing, I wasn't interested in any more art but I hung around till about 10pm when the event closed.

I left the gallery in the GAZ 69, I got back to the Hotel Tver feeling disappointed about the night. I had nothing; I didn't even meet with the asset. How was I going to find the agent? How was I going to solve my mission and get the fuck out of Russia? I missed Carla, I wallowed yet again, and I had my head in my hand. I was already failing from the beginning, that's not a very good omen. I had my room key in my hand and it fell while I wallowed and as I bent down to pick it, and a small paper fell from the breast pocket of my suit as well as my pocket square. I picked both up, I didn't think too much of the paper, I wanted to throw it away but from some reason, I just decided to check what paper it was. It was a note from Daria Iyanov. I didn't know what she had written on it, her address maybe, a number to call to get her but as I opened it, it dawned on me that I had been with the asset the whole time. On the note, she wrote "dresser, inside the suit bag of the brown suit". I rushed into the room, locked the door behind me and quickly opened the dresser, opened the suit bad and I saw a brown file. Daria was the asset and she had delivered information to me. I had to continue from here on out. I shouldn't look for her, her parts complete. My mission was looking up finally. I could leave Russia sooner than I expected.

CHAPTER TWENTY THREE: THE ENCOUNTER

I picked up the file, I needed to sit down before going through this, I checked through all the windows, to ensure no one was on my tail. I sat down close to a lamp, I had directed the head of the lamp close to the file, and I didn't want to miss a single detail. I opened the file and boldly typed as header was Harold Pike. That was the agent I came to find. Where do I look for him, maybe this file was going to answer the basic questions?

I opened the file, it had a brief of his mission, when he arrived, the information he had given and when he fell off grid. Those were information I had already, I needed to know where he was or where he was going to be? I was still reading the file and I saw something that would be very useful to me. The place he was when last he contacted the asset was Litvinki. I knew at this point that that was where I should start my search. It was almost 11:00pm and I clearly wasn't tired. I changed into something simple and headed down to the bar for a drink.

I was doing everything right I thought to myself, I had met the asset and I was on course to find the agent on ground, it wasn't as hard as I feared. I could be out of here in no time. I just needed to find Litvinki, study the grounds, and put myself in his shoe, where would I be hiding if I were him. I thought I had it all figured out but it wasn't to be. I noticed a band of guys drinking late at night. My eyes would occasionally meet with them but I brushed it off to the side. I wasn't the only one who had the right to drink late at night after all.

The guys did look suspicious, but I was not going to concern myself with them. I ignored them and walked back to my room.

I went back to the room, laid down on the bed, I was fighting the desire to pick up the phone and call my parents so I could hear from Carla but I didn't know if anyone was on to me. I had to maintain a low profile. I needed a few more days at Tver to finish my mission and go back. I just needed to begin my search in the morning and I'd be a step closer to going back home. I forced myself to sleep with the conviction that the sooner it was morning, the sooner I could start looking for Pike and the sooner I could get the fuck out of this place. That wasn't the case, the night wouldn't end, I woke up in between, a lot times until eventually I decided to stay awake until it was morning or I fell asleep genuinely. I laid there unable to sleep until it was morning, almost daybreak, thoughts running through my mind. I slept off eventually, woke up at around 7:00am. The timing was perfect. I got dressed, wore a coat and a heard warmer as I left the room.

It was time to go out there to do what I was here for. I had to find Harold fast. I wasn't comfortable knowing the nature of my mission in Russia. Litvinki, a small district in Southern Tver. It was a simple town, didn't boast much structures but it looked peaceful. It was more a suburb than an urban city. The residents knew themselves personally, I could tell because as I drove through the district, they related closely with themselves. It made me stand out more than I'd have loved to.

I didn't know where to start from and I didn't want eyes to be on me. I went into town like a tourist with a camera and a notepad. I tried to stay away as much from the open streets to remain as Anonymous as I could be.

Nothing seemed off about the town, but I knew it was no fluke that it was mentioned in the file I received from the asset. I would see something if I stayed there long enough. I checked into a motel to spend the night. I had been noticing strange movements around me the entire time I was in Litvinki like someone was following me but who would know who I was and what I was doing here. I brushed it off as being paranoid but I trotted carefully. It was room 16 at Otel praga. I was curled up on end of the bed as I tried to put my thoughts through my next move. Time went by without me even noticing. It was at 2:00 am, I heard footsteps walking across the hallway, from the sounds, they were two men wearing boots as the sounds of their feet were heavy. They were talking but the tune was low. They had heavy Russian accent but as they approached my door, their voices became more audible.

I had the idea that they were heading for my room but just as the sound was right in front of my door, it started to fade as though they continued walking, and I relaxed a little. I guess I was being paranoid but clearly, I wasn't just as I got up from the bed to confirm if the door was locked, they opened fire on my room. The sound of gunshots filling the air and the damages that the bullets were causing inside my room brought me back to earth, they didn't go away. They just wanted me to think they did. I crawled under the bed, brought out my berretta 92 handgun. We had another rodeo to attend together. I checked the cartridge and it was loaded.

I knew I had to do something now or I was going to be in real trouble. I waited for them to finish shooting, I knew they were going to try to enter to see if I was dead, I came out from underneath the bed, I saw the door knob twirl and I knew they were trying to enter, I looked behind me, I could make my escape through the window. As they attempted to open the door, I shot multiple times straight at the door, the barrel moving forward and backwards as hot lead followed each other out of the nozzle. I heard a shout suggesting that I had hit someone and the other reacted in Russian trying to tend to the wounded. It was now or never for me. I broke through the window, jumping out of the room. I sustained a few glass cut but that would be nothing compared to what I'd get from these guys who were out to kill me. They had adopted a shoot first ask questions later approach, clearly they weren't here for a chit chat or anything.

While I tried to escape, I had a cut on my left arm from jumping out of a motel window, I ran into the streets where I saw two SUV parked, they were Ford, if I remember correctly, it was the Bronco, the ford bronco, black and the occupants were all dressed In black with ski masks. I knew instantaneously that the guys that just shot at me were part of this gang. I couldn't avoid them as they had seen me. I ran in the opposite direction trying to find some cover. I was saved by the fact that they weren't trigger ready. I had just a berretta with me, I couldn't have a prolonged shootout with guys with automatic rifles, all six of them. I needed a place evade them and take cover. My mission had been blown wide open. "Who could have possibly known I was a spy? It was top secret even in Britain. Somebody had fucked me over. It had to be the directors of one of the agencies but why? Were thy trying to sell Britain too these fuckers? What if it was something I did that made them know I wasn't an art enthusiast but an agent. This wasn't the right time to be thinking too much, I just needed to stay alive a little longer and I'd have the answers to these questions".

I gave them a head start and they couldn't chase me with their cars. I snuck into an alley, hid behind a waste bin. It was then when I was a little calm that I realized that I had been hit when they opened fire at my room door. I had been bleeding the whole time I was running. I was still bleeding even now. I checked my berretta to see how many rounds I had left. Just five. It didn't make any sense to me, why send me out here if they were just going to kill me. If they didn't want the information Harold was carrying to come out, they'd just have invested enough in killing him, why send me out here just to kill me? I thought to myself as I felt my body loosing energy as blood came out of my gunshot wound. I knew I had to stay awake, if I fainted, I'd be giving them the chance to capture and kill me. I applied more pressure. I knew that from here on out, they couldn't see me because if they did, I'd be dead for sure.

I managed to stay there for a while but I couldn't forever, I heard footsteps coming in my direction, I knew I was fucked, I didn't even have ammunition and I was already weak. The steps weren't much, it was just one and it wasn't heavy, whoever it was wasn't wearing a boot, that didn't match the guys that were out to kill me. Maybe it was a friend or a different assassin. Conflicted, I decided to just get up, if they were a threat shoot but if they weren't, just play it cool. It took a lot of courage but I got up eventually with my berretta at hand trigger ready pointing straight at whoever it was and it was the last person I expected to see, it Was Dariya Iyanov. How did she find me? How did she know I was in trouble? I had even more questions now than I had before but now, I was just glad to see her.

"What are you doing here?" I asked, "You don't look like you need an explanation as to why I am going to save your life". I was weary of a lot of things at this moment. The only person I trusted was my own self but I needed her help anyways. "Follow me, my car is not far from here". I agreed and followed her anyways but just as we entered her cars, the guys attempting to kill me, showed up just behind us. They opened fire at the car. Round after round hitting the boot and the rear windshield of the car. I ducked to avoid being hit as did she. She started the car as we drove away. I knew they couldn't catch up as their trucks were far away from the point where she picked me up but I was wrong. As we drove away, I looked behind and saw their Ford trucks picking them up, ready for a chase. "You think you can go a little faster?" she looked at me with a devilish smirk on her face she screamed "hold on to something pretty boy". She increased her grip on the steering wheel as she stepped on the accelerator pedal. I fastened my seat belt and held on for dear life, the Pontiac firebird 1980 responded almost immediately. She hit speeds of over 150km/h. It was shocking as the car could go a maximum 190km/h.

She had a lust for action and she had concealed that lust ever so carefully at the auction but right now it was out there, the beauty I had seen in her eyes prior had given way to action and adventure. She turned on the car stereo, she cranked the volume to the highest it could get, she looked at me and screamed "this way you don't hear the sounds of the gun shots when they shoot at us". That was clearly not true besides the fear of gunshots wasn't the sound they made but the damage they caused. We were in an open road and the ford Bronco was catching up with us pretty quick we had to do something about that because if they got too close, they'd shoot at us. She knew all too well and she had a plan of action, I didn't know what it was but I knew I wouldn't like it. She pushed down the clutch while pulling on the handbrake and took her foot off the gas as she flipped the steering wheel completely to the right. The tires screeched as she made a hard turn to the right. I thought we were going to die, there's no way we could make that turn but she had skills. The car turned hard right taking us into a busy interstate.

They made the turn as well but it gave us more time to evade, plus they couldn't shoot at us in here. They were cars in between. I liked Daria when I saw her in a dress all dolled but this badass version of her was amazing. Added to the fact that she is literally saving her my life, she was doing it looking like actual James Bond if he were female anyways. I was bleeding out but the pressure I kept on it was probably what was keeping me alive.

"You need help else you'll bleed out and die". I knew that was the truth, but I couldn't die, at least not yet. I had a wife and kid to go back to. "I'm fine don't worry too much about me, and focus on the road". "You talk a big game, you didn't look very big when you were behind that bin waiting for death", she said as she laughed. I tried to return the laugh but I was in too much pain than I expected. It was over, the chase or so I thought. We both realized that there was nowhere to drive to as traffic was locked. The express way led to Moscow, and it was congested. It was Russian Independence Day and people from around the country were heading to Moscow. We came down from the car and made way by foot. I looked behind and saw them checking the car to see if we were still there. I was drawing her back. My blood was leaving a trail for them to follow. I needed to do something about that. I was thinking when I heard her call me. She had taken control of a bike, I didn't know where she got it from until I saw a guy shouting and cussing in Russian. The screams attracted them but we sped off.

I don't know how that made them feel but I was sure they thought among themselves prior that they had already gotten me but it seems I was the only one who got anyone. She took me to a small house out in the woods, it seemed pretty off grid. This was how she had managed to remain anonymous the whole time, I thought to myself. I was happy to still be breathing but the second we got into the house, I realized I was too weak to speak or even move, I could feel life leaving me, it seemed the pressure I applied on the gunshot wound wasn't enough, the blood stain on my shirt had grown significantly suggesting I was bleeding a lot. I tried to call out to Daria who was standing in front of me but I could barely speak. She was going to get something from the kitchen when I fainted. She turned round when she heard the sound of my boots against the wooden floor.

It was pitch black, I was standing in nothing. There was an endless space but nothing was there but me, I could talk but there was no one there with me. Is this how it feels to be dead? I couldn't remain here forever. There was nothing here. I'd be miserable. I saw Col Harry a long way away in the emptiness, I tried to run towards him but I couldn't. My feet weren't contacting any sort of floor. It was like I was floating but I couldn't control my movement to get to him. He was fading away little by little, I stretched my hand hoping I could get to him but I couldn't. I gave up and retracted my hand but just at the moment, he appeared right in front of me and as I tried to hold on to him, he said to me "you are not supposed to be here. There's a lot waiting for you out there". I didn't understand where he was talking about. I tried to respond but words wouldn't come out. The darkness began to fade away and a bright light took over.

I opened my eyes to the bright morning light. It was day, I wasn't dead. I had been given another chance to see out my days or at least fulfil my mission before death came. My wound had been dressed and my bloodied clothes replaced. I woke up but Daria wasn't in the room with me. I went out in search of her and I met her sitting at the porch at the back of the house. She had a bottle of wine and two glasses on the table like she had entertained a guest or she was hoping to entertain one. As I walked out heading towards her, she said" I thought you'd never wake up, you've been out for a while you know" "how long?" I asked. "A while. Sit, drink with me". This was clearly no time to be drinking, I was just almost killed but I needed that drink anyways, so I obliged her. "Who were those guys and why did they want me dead?" She looked at me "I don't know who they are, but why they want you dead? In your line of work, everyone wants you dead". It made sense, I was in their country to uncover national secrets so it was no wonder why they wanted to kill me but how they knew who I was, that I couldn't understand.

"I barely just got to Russia, I'm sure nobody should know who I am. They knew I was an agent. That means there is a mole in British intelligence" I said out loud "or you just did a lousy job at keeping your identity hidden" she cut in quickly. That's a possibility but I'd have to at least done something for them to find out who I was. "If you count staying in the hotel all the time and attending the gallery as being lousy then yes, I have been pretty lousy" I responded. "I'm sorry, I didn't mean it that way" she said with remorse written all over her face. I figured she was just being tense from having multiple gunmen shoot at her sporadically. "It's okay, you might be right, I might have slipped up somehow and I've ended up putting you in my problems. I guess I'm really fucking useless". "No need to be too hard on yourself, it's never easy this job" she responded. I nodded.

I had compromised her clearly, she couldn't remain an asset for British intelligence in Russia anymore, and she had to go out of commission once this mission ends because her identity had been compromised. I looked at her looking ever so beautiful even in the face of uncertainty. "How'd you know I was in trouble?" I asked, she smiled and said "I am part of an operation called Guardian angel. We aren't just assets on the ground, we protect agents when necessary. A lot of agents had lost their lives in service to their country and there was need for support while on duty. Our operation is classified that's why you've never heard of it, I'm not even supposed to tell you but since we almost tasted death together, I figured what the heck. The second you came down from the flight from London, I had been on to you. When I met you at the auction, I noticed there were some others unto you as well so I knew I had to stick around and lucky for you, I was at the right place at the right time". I owed her a lot. "Thank you", I said "you don't have to, I am just doing my service to my country".

"What's next for me now?" I asked her, she looked at me with an expression that suggested she felt my pain "you are not a deserter, you should finish your mission, find the agent you came for and take the information back to HQ. Don't worry about me, I'll be fine". That sounded like a plan but where was I going to start from if my cover had been blown at Tver. I was going to sneak back in the town, maintain a low profile and still go on my mission. At least I know now that I have a guardian angel looking after me, I wasn't alone, I couldn't keep putting her in trouble. "I'm going to leave, I just needed a little time for my injuries to heal and I'll be out of your skin". She looked at me "take your time. This place is secure, but I'm going to have to leave you on your own. Everything you need is available. Just be ok". We finished the drink in silence and just sat down there for a while. She left me there that morning and I didn't know where she was going to or if she'd ever come back but I was grateful for all she had done.

CHAPTER TWENTY FOUR: CONTACT

It took a while for me but in five days I was fine. I had to leave in search of Harold Pike. I got dressed, check the garage to find a Porsche 911, I was sure Daria wouldn't mind if I borrowed it. I didn't know where I was going to start searching but I had to. I didn't know where this safe house was but if I followed the road we came back with, I'd be on the interstate and I'd on my way back to Tver. I was going to save Ronald Pike but one thing bothered me, will Daria Iyanov still be unto me or had she done enough.

The interstate was clear and in no time, I was in Tver. I couldn't go back to the motel I was but I had to lay low. I hadn't checked into any motel. I was just on the road the entire day, when it was night time, I entered a bar, it was quiet, unexpected in a cold town like Tver but it was best for me. Had my drink, it was getting late, people were starting to come around, I had to leave before someone recognized me. I didn't see the faces of my pursuers after all so they could be right next to me and I wouldn't know but they would. I left the bar and booked a hotel nearby. This time, I was being really discreet. I couldn't have people chasing after me yet again.

I did same thing night after night again, hoping I'd stumble into something, someone, anyone that was either Harold Pike or will lead me to Harold Pike but nothing was forthcoming. The mission started on a high note and I thought it would continue that way but it had fallen off grid. I wasn't going anywhere with my search. I was never going to see Harold this way. I decided in my heart that I'd return to the safe house and try to communicate with HQ about proceedings before demanding orders because if I continued this way, I was going to eventually end up dead.

I was on my usual daily search. The search has spanned for weeks and now months, I needed to contact Daria or HQ. I needed new orders. I was certain I wasn't going to find Harold at Litvinki or even Tver in general. I was retreating for the night.

I saw two Ford bronco, they looked all too familiar. I didn't want to believe it but it was the gang that attacked me. I parked the Porsche carefully out of sight, I waited to confirm. I didn't see their faces but I could tell from their structures or something. Five guys came out from the vehicles, heavily armed yet again. It seems that is what they do, they take out targets. They were some kill squad or something and a really tenacious one at that. If I was going to survive this mission, I had to avoid them. They probably have something against me for killing one of their own and for attempting to uncover Russian national secrets.

What were they doing here anyways and why were they armed? I was eager to find out but I waited none the less for the action to fade out. They went in, there wasn't much shooting, but people came running out of the bar into the streets. They came out shortly after and drove off. I needed to see who they were after, I went in, the place was completely empty, the bartender had been shot, and he was dead. I checked his pocket for Identification, he was Russian Yuri Krishikov. I don't know why he was killed but I couldn't stay to find out, Harold Pike wasn't the reason for the shooting, I left the bar in a hurry, entered the Porsche and drove off.

I was running low on patience, my wife was pregnant, I didn't even know for how long and I was in Russia playing James Bond. At least Bond would have solved the problem but here I was, not a clue in the world what to do next, I was nowhere close to finding Harold. Heck the only way I could find him was if he found me first.

I retired back to my motel and as I walked in, I found a file on the bed. Who kept it there, were they on to me again? Do I have to leave this motel as well because I clearly didn't want another attack? The envelope on the bed made me a bit worried. Maybe it was a message from Daria. I needed to talk to her, I hadn't seen her in a while and I was feeling lost. I opened the envelope, and the content gave me hope yet again. It was a message from Harold Pike. He was clearly in Litvinki, I didn't need to go back to the safe house at least, and I didn't have to go back alone. I could take him with me and we'd be one step closer to closing this case. I was awfully excited seeing the message of a middle aged man I had never seen in my life but the joy was only necessary.

The message read "you have to get the fuck out of here, you are not safe, and I am not safe as well. If nothing seems suspicious to you about all this then you are clearly not looking at the right things. I don't even know if I can trust you, I don't know if I can trust anyone. You shouldn't either. Meeting me is only a recipe for disaster. You not finding me is the only thing that has kept you alive this far. Just give up on finding me and stay alive. What you are going to find out is bigger than you think. If you make it out of Russia alive, you might not back in England". I didn't understand what he was going on about. Of course, there had been incidences where I questioned authorities but Daria made it clear that it must have been something I did. Why would the UK sell him out, why would they want us dead? He must have seen a lot while here I thought to myself. It's driving the man insane. I had to find him none the less. I figured he was the one that they went looking for at the bar. Maybe they might have missed him and took their frustrations out on the innocent bartender.

I wish he would have put in that message a way to reach him. It was an annoying habit of all agents not to want you to contact them but for them to be the ones to contact you. It was part of the job but it was becoming a serious bother. The envelope made me relax a little. It wasn't Daria like I wanted it to be but it wasn't the people that wanted me dead whoever they are. I could rest easy that night at the very least. He was alive and that meant I could find him and leave Russia soon. I was going to keep trying. Maybe if he notices my efforts, he'd contact me again. I was about to place the note back in the envelope when I saw a small writing at the back. It was an address, a date and a time. I figured he knew I wasn't going to back out from finding him so he gave me directions anyway.

I laid on the bed with the note he sent me in my hands. Why can't I trust anyone, our contacts were all that we had. Without them, we'd be dead. Not finding him was the only reason I was still alive? What the bollocks did that even mean? I could barely sleep. I was supposed to meet him at an abandoned church in south Litvinki by 7:00 pm the next night. It was all too shady. What if it wasn't even

Harold? What if it was those guys who wanted me dead? I had to be really careful what I did next. I couldn't leave it all to chance. I couldn't overthink anything. It'd work out, I was sure of that. I slept off in the hope that I'd find Harold, convince him to go back to. England with me and all would be fine. It seemed a plan but what I was going to face would change even my own opinion about going back home.

I couldn't trust anyone was the biggest concern I had with the note. I needed to ensure that I was meeting him alone. I had a gut feeling that someone was on to me again but I wasn't sure. I needed to be careful.

He had managed himself very well before I can into the picture. I needed to ensure that meeting him wasn't going to be the end of both of us or either of us. I was so conflicted right now. This was one of those moments when I would just lie down on Carla's laps and have her talk my problems away or at the very least talk to the prime minister and get advice. I missed working at Downing Street. It wasn't eventful but at least it wasn't life threatening. I miss Carla's strawberry pie, I missed my mom's cooking. I missed spending time with Carla as we both walked back from the coffee shop after a hard day's work. I miss home and I wanted to go back but I knew I was already in too deep to just run away. I could go back and be at peace when this was done. I slept off but as usual in my line of work, no sleep is ever comfortable.

The night was short and it was morning again. The big day. Today was going to play a huge part in what happens next and I was ready for it. I had my berretta on the table. I needed to get it set because it might be needed where I was going to. I needed to be more ready than ever. I hadn't come this far to just get killed now. I was going to make it out, that was my resolve and I was going to take Harold with me regardless. We were going to walk into London and unmask whatever was going there. I knew it wasn't going to be that easy but I was determined. Something dirty was going on in British intelligence. It was either that or Harold Pike was just paranoid. Either way, I needed to be ready for what was to come later this night.

CHAPTER TWENTY FIVE: DESPAIR OF BETRAYAL

The day went by peacefully, I had to ensure I wasn't followed, I had damaged the file he sent to me. I couldn't put both our lives at risk. I drove the Porsche to a bar along east side Litvinki, I parked and went in like I wanted a drink or something, and I made way through the back door just in case anybody had been on my trail. I walked a while before I found a cab headed down south. I didn't understand why we had to meet in a place so hidden. We could meet in public and try to blend with the crowd but I was sure he knew what he was doing. I had a lot of questions and a lot to say to him. Beginning with "what the fuck is going on?"

It was a long drive to south Litvinki but by the time I finally arrived, it was 6:57pm. I waited just across the road from the abandoned church at a restaurant. I needed to see if I was going in alone or someone else was going in with me. I watched carefully until it was about 7:10 pm. I saw someone come out from the door walking quickly away from the church, maybe that was Harold, I followed him, I said nothing, and I made no sound.

He made a hard left into a dark alley and I followed. I finally caught up to him where he was seated waiting for me. "Smart move kid". I didn't see where he was at the time but I was startled when I heard the voice, I tried to figure out where it was coming from, "how did he know I had been following him? I was being really discreet" I thought to myself. "I noticed you when you came out of the restaurant, I must say your stealth was amazing. I could barely hear you or anything".

I was flattered but that wasn't why we were here "I had questions, a lot of them and I need answers" I walked up to him "how did you know I was an agent and I was looking for you". "I'm an agent like you lad and I have my ways" he responded. That was true but I wasn't done with him yet "what's going on? Why did you go off grid? Why can't I trust anyone?" The questions kept coming and all he could do was smile. He clenched his fist and adjusted his cap properly as he was about to answer "you were sent here to find me or uncover a plot about overtaking Luxembourg and some other European nations like I was but the plot is way bigger than that. It doesn't end there, it goes way beyond that. Russia is teaming up with some European power houses to form a super government capable of seizing the entirety of Europe. You might think that's pretty big but I think the idea has been sold to the prime minister in recent times". The moment I heard the prime minister, I was a lot more concerned. I wanted to know if he consented to forming a super government at the expense of smaller nations.

Harold saw my focus and smiled. He continued none the less "the English prime minister turned down the proposal to form a super government but there are some members of the opposition party that are opened to the idea of a British super government. Ordinarily the prime minister has the say in those kind of situations but I picked up on a troubling information that the Russians have teamed up with some English officials to take out the prime minister and place someone in power that will buy into the idea". "Take out the prime minister? You mean kill the prime minister?" He nodded. I couldn't believe it, so they were actually forces in Britain that didn't want us to bring this information home. This was huge. We had to tell someone, anyone.

"Why then did you go off grid, you could have sent this information back home", he continued " I wanted to but like I just said, there's so much rot in British politics and it's found its way into the security service. I got this information intercepting a call from the lead researcher in a military research facility at Tver. I overheard him talking about it and he laughed it off like it didn't mean anything when he said it. I don't know who is on the other end of the call but I couldn't go back home. I'd be walking right into their hands. I told you in the note I sent to you, if they can't get you here in Russia, they'd get you when you get back to England. Accepting this mission meant accepting certain death. I realized that a while ago and I was just going to go off grid for a while and then go far away from here". It made sense his decision to go missing but for how long could he hide from the Russians as well as the English?

"I told you not meeting me was the only thing keeping you alive but you chose to throw that away". I responded immediately "I hadn't even met you when they started making attempts at me. I have been shot at, chased and all around Russia since I entered the God damn country". He smiled and shook his head "but they hadn't gotten you. Do you think they are that bad a shot? They were waiting for you to find me and they'd kill us both. It's like killing two birds with a stone". I never thought of it that way "why then did you arrange to meet me?" I asked. He continued "I had been alone for a while and I knew I didn't stand a chance but with you around, we have a decent chance of getting out of here alive, somehow". I nodded. "We will get out of this place alive. I have a lot waiting for me back in England".

"It's simple what we have to do next, contact Daria Iyanov, if she can get us through to HQ, I know a few people I can trust to get us out of here". He raised his head in shock "didn't you hear anything I just said about trusting no one?" He was still talking when Daria showed up where we were. He became very scared when he saw her, he got up and pointed his gun at her "whoa whoa calm down, she's with us" I tried to get him to drop the gun, but he wouldn't "you are a fool, she's not with us. You never wonder how she always shows up just before you get fucked. How she guarantees you that no one is fucking the plan up? She's with them you fucker!" It made absolute sense now, I turned towards Daria "how the fuck did you know I needed help?" She brought out her handgun and before I could say another word, she shot me right in the shoulder. The bullet went straight into my right shoulder causing me to scream in pain, blood spilled on the floor and wall, I held on to the gunshot wound as blood kept dripping from it. Immediately the same guys that attempted to kill me showed up right behind her.

We could run away but turning our backs to them would spell the end "great job boss" one of them said talking to Daria. "Boss? You work with them? I thought you were an agent for the UK?" With a sinister smile in her face, her gun still pointing at me "I'm Russian honey, I spent the majority of my life in London doesn't make me English. Your agency thought they had an asset in me, but I was doubling as an agent for Russia as well getting information from the English as an asset in Russia. Smart right? I'm going to kill the two of you here and I'm sure a lot of rewards await me when I do from the Russian secret services in Moscow and the British intelligence as well".

I had no plan, I was out of option, in the past one week, I had been shot twice, have had near death experiences, had been betrayed and I had been sent on a suicide mission. If death were to come today, I would take it. My time in the secret service had been anything but peaceful but Harold wasn't going down without a fight, it was dark, and he had unpinned a grenade. While I spoke with Daria, he threw the grenade and there was an explosion, he hadn't warned me about it but had made sure he threw it away from me so I wouldn't be really affected by the explosion.

The shockwave from the grenade sent everyone tumbling to the ground, he was up as he was the farthest from the blast, he got up and pulled me up and we both ran into the alley. He seemed to know the area and before long we were almost out of sight. We took a secret path that led us back into the abandoned church that he just left. It wasn't the best route to go through, but it had gotten us safely away from our pursuers. We needed to lay low. I was bleeding all over the place, he tore the sleeves of his shirt and tied the injury to stop the bleeding. "I'll get you to my place, fix you up and we both Leave Tver. We have to find a way to make it back to England somehow. "We have contact to HQ somehow. I know you said something about trusting no one but I have a real relationship with the prime minister and I'm sure he doesn't want to die. He'd definitely help us" he was shocked at the level of my naivety. "We can't do that, you won't get through to the prime minister, the call would have to go through one of those people we can't trust. I know it's hard for you to believe that there are people inside the intelligence agency that would do this but there are. You either have to be careful or you get killed".

As we got up to leave the cathedral, we heard footsteps approaching the small door that led us back into the building. "I think it's them, we should get out of here" Harold cut in as he led me out of the abandoned church. We rushed out and by the time we got outside, we found Daria's blue Pontiac Firebird, she had repaired the damages from the last shootout. We both jumped in the car, and I drove off. They followed but we were too far away for them to meet up.

I never thought in my wildest dreams that Daria was a double agent. She was our only link to HQ and with her gone, there was no way we could communicate with HQ. We had been cut off from the world. We couldn't leave Russia by flight as they'd have soldiers stationed in every airport in the country, we could leave by sea or by train, but it'd be really difficult to avoid security. We needed to lay low for a while and allow the dust to settle a little bit. First, we had to ditch Daria's car and get a new one. "You can't really trust anyone can you?" I said with a grim expression, he looked at me "that's the first rule of espionage". He continued "we are highly replaceable. One wrong move and you are out. I didn't do anything, but someone had to take this mission and its consequences and to cover their horrible acts, they threw in another agent, you. We mean nothing to the men and women that sit on those executive chairs. We are out here dying and killing for our country, and they are there taking the glory of it all. It's never fair but I'll give my blood and sweat for England". He had the same resolve I had. "Let's rid England of these unwanted entities then". He smiled and nodded his head as we drove off.

CHAPTER TWENTY-SIX: STEP BACK

We had to claw our way back from the crannies of Russia to England. Harold had been hiding for so long but hiding would make you a prisoner of your own fear all your life. I wasn't going to live like that. I was going to take back my life, I was going to clean the system but first I needed to know who was dirty and who was clean. I will return home and save England once again. To do that however, I needed to find Daria, she knew the roots that needed to be uprooted but I was dead sure she wasn't going to willingly tell us. We had to pry it from her cold lifeless corpse if need be because without it, going back to England would be like walking into a den of lions without any protection and it wouldn't be like Daniel in the Bible, it would be messy. We dropped off her Pontiac firebird at a parking lot, stole someone else's Ford Mariciato and left for Harold's hide out.

I had been in Saudi where I saw soldiers defending their country to the death, I saw terrorists die for a cause that they believed in but right here in Russia, it was a different thing all together. I learnt here that loyalty meant nothing to some people like it meant to me. They'd sell their souls to the devil for a little change but that's the problem, they'd have gotten away with it if they didn't involve me in all of this. I was an agent who wanted to live his life in peace but I'm going to be a torn in their flesh. I will not rest until I purge the system of dirty agents. I had always had the resolve to fight for England before anything else and this was the biggest threat. I was fighting for England, but my enemies were disguised as England herself.

Harold's hideout was a dump, he lived in conditions nobody striving hard to protect the integrity of their nation should ever have to live. It was an abandoned building which he shared with other homeless people. It used to be an old church that burned down under mysterious circumstances. Why it hasn't been renovated, nobody knew but it was pretty smart of Harold, to hide in plain sight. The smell that rippled through the air inside the building was horrible, it smelled like rotten flesh, you could hear the floors creak as you walked on them. It was almost a warning and a cry for help, it was long overdue for demolition, but nobody moved an inch. The cracks on the walls stretched from foundation to roof and all the inhabitants knew that the building could collapse at any time, but it was better than living in the streets. Harold had secured for himself the cosiest spot in the entire building. It was a destroyed room but compared to other rooms in the house, it was cosy. He had a small bed and a pile of magazines, a cloth that he hung across the door giving some sort of privacy. I was utterly disgusted at how much he had been left alone. "Is this the same fate that awaits all agents? Would we all be left alone at the very first sight of trouble? Was this our worth to the secret service?" Resentment swelled within me, but I had to tone it down. If I get too angry, I might decide to walk away from all this, and two things would happen if I walked away. I could never go home and the people I love and care about, Carla, the prime minister, my parents, Carla's parents will all be in danger. I couldn't have that.

We both sat down on the small bed, he gave me something to drink but I didn't feel comfortable where we were, so I turned it down. I could never accept living like this. We had to devise a plan to get out of here as quickly as possible. He looked lost internally, outwardly, he had managed to maintain his sanity but internally, he was a mess. He could do with a warm bath, a change of clothes and some decent treatment but he could only get all that when we finish here. "You have any family?" I asked trying to establish connection outside of work. He looked at me like he didn't know the answer to the question I just asked but he did know, he had an answer to the question, but it was really difficult for him to say what was in his mind "I do have a family or should I say had. I am sure that they must have moved on without me. I mean I've been gone a while. I have a wife and two lads, Higgins and Hughes. Higgins would be 9 and Hughes 7. My boys are growing up without a father. I thought I'd be done with this by now and go back home and be with my family. I never saw this possibility". He said as tears rolled down his cheeks. He had been gone a while, he had to go home and see his family. "What about you, you got a family?" He threw the question back at me. I had a sad story but mine was nowhere near his, I shouldn't show too many emotions, it'd break his spirit even more, I had to be strong for the both of us. "I have a pregnant wife, no kid yet but expecting", he smiled a little "congratulations. It's the best feeling in the world, having a kid". I didn't know much about that, but I do know that knowing alone that Carla was pregnant made me so happy I could burst out of joy, I could imagine how I'd feel when she gives birth to a child, to my child.

I've been here almost two months and with every day I spend in Russia, I miss the moments I could spend making my pregnant wife feel like a queen. We had to leave. "I have a plan". He looked and his eyes glowed, he was excited, he knew with a plan of action, we had taken a step towards going back home "well, get on with its Lad" he said with joy. I could see the rays of hope shining ever so gently on his bristled skin, the hunger to reunite with his family partnered with my supposed plan made him visibly happy. He stood up from the wrinkled bed that he was lying on, eager to hear me out. "There's only one way we can get out of here and that is either we carry Daria along or we kill Daria, but the only way is with Daria out of the way. With her out of commission, we could sneak into England, I have connections with the prime minister, and I could warn him of the plot we had uncovered and maybe with some help, he can discover whoever is behind it".

He looked down trying to gather his thoughts and maybe suppress his excitement. My plan clearly didn't give him the thrill he had expected, it had so many loopholes, we were living a lot to chance and when you do that, you meet your end, he was thinking about how to improve the plan as was I. Some minutes later, he jumped out of the bed "I've got it!" he did look like he was on to something and boy, was I excited. "What is it, mate?" I enquired happily. He was pacing around the room trying to tie up all loose ends with the plan before he told me what it was. He stopped at a point and then I realized he was ready to tell me what the plan was. He started talking "while undercover at the research facility to discover what weapons they were making at Tver, I met another agent in a separate mission, he was there for something called project x" I raised my brows "I reckon you have heard of it?" He asked, I was already buying his plan "yes, I have, the prime minister spoke about it to me just before I left London. Some sort of truth serum or something". He continued "I wish it were that simple, it didn't make you say the truth, it places the victim in untold agony, none like the human body can contain or manage, it won't kill the victim but the pain could last forever as long as the antidote isn't administered, they'd be in absolute pain and until they answered what was asked, the antidote won't be given".

That was inhumane I thought but it's the Russians, there's nothing they won't do for power and control. He wasn't done telling me about the plan. "The plan is really risky, but we have to contact that agent. Have no fear, I can get to him, there's no telling how he'd react to meeting me after a while, I don't know what Daria might have said to him but it's a chance we should take". It was a decent plan, but I had to ask "did you tell this agent about the stain in British intelligence? Why would he help you still if you had gone off grid?" He didn't expect me to ask but he had to answer anyways "I didn't tell him the context of my findings, I just told him my handler has been killed and that I couldn't get through to HQ, he tried to connect me through his but I knew giving out my location to HQ would mean my death anyways so I stayed away from him as much as I could". I didn't understand his decision "why didn't you tell him?" he looked at the floor, clenched his fist as he continued "I could have told him, but that might have affected his mission. I won't lie to you, despite what's going on in the British intelligence, there is a genuine scare in Russia and if we are ever going to come close to fixing it, we need all agents active.

I wasn't going to let my problems put millions of English lives in jeopardy". He had a point but I still didn't get why someone in so much danger would still put the lives of the people going after his first. He looked at my puzzled expression "there are only a handful of people who want me dead, I couldn't forget about the millions of innocents in England". I knew at the point that he had genuine love for his nation. That's the kind of man I want to be. He continued, "getting access to project x would be tough but I'm sure he can get us the serum and its antidote. Once we have that, we can get Daria, get her to tell us everybody involved with this in London, then we can go back to the prime minister. That's the only way we make it out of this alive".

The plan made absolute sense but we needed evidence against them if not, it'd just be two agents accusing decorated agents and nobody would take us seriously, they'd just lock us up. Regardless of the relationship I had with the prime minister, it wasn't going to be enough when I just show up and accuse some of his closest associates. We needed to find a way to involve the agents in Britain, first we find out who they were and then we can stop them. I had a lot of questions but asking them would put doubts in both our hearts, so I just had to keep them to myself. We'll solve every problem as they come. A plan thought by two cornered agents was never going to be a good plan anyways.

We had a framework; it was time for us to hunt down Daria. She had always had us in her sights but now we had to find her and quick. It was going to be tough; she always had her goons around but if we could find her, get some sort of confession out of her, we could well be on our way to going back home. Finding Daria wasn't going to be too hard but capturing her, I couldn't say. All we had to do was find the guys she rolled with, and we'd find her. Luckily for us, they don't do a very good job at hiding themselves. They were always at bars at night, causing trouble. We didn't need to get all of them, just one and we'd be fine. For this to work, we needed weapons, lots of them. Harold knee just where we could get some.

There was an old gun's dealer just down the block, he could get us what we wanted. I had the money to pay and Harold the connection to buy guns from a Russian gun dealer. Again, I had a functioning partner. It reminded me a lot of Hassan at Saudi Arabia. This time, I wasn't going to let my partner die. I was going to deliver him to his wife in one piece and alive. We spent the next few days strategizing, it's not like we knew the playing field as well as the enemy, but it was better going in with a plan than just going in blind. I had spent time in that abandoned building, I was feeling very uncomfortable. One thing was different though, the inhabitants dwelled together in peace. A couple of times while there, I had seen them protect each other and provide for each other irrespective of decent. I figured that was why Harold remained there, they all loved like they never ever noticed he was British. They could protect him from danger like he was their own blood.

We were ready somewhat for the first phase of our push back. Harold left early to meet up with the agent to get the serum like he had suggested he wanted to use on Daria. I stayed behind at the hideout. The whole time, I was hopeful that he'd return alive. I thought it'd have been better if we went together but he opted to go alone as the two of us out in the open was a bigger target than one. We both knew Daria and her goons would be out looking for us and the only way to beat them at their own game was to maintain a low profile and strike when the odds were completely in our favour as they had the advantages of numbers and ammunition. We had to think with our heads and not our hearts. I watched the roads from the cracked window at the hideout. It was in a small town with a lot of bars. It stood just there in the open streets. I reckoned nobody would ever suspect that we were hiding in plain sight.

Harold has been gone the whole day, I was starting to get worried, but I needed to have a little faith in the man, he had kept himself alive all these while with little or no resources, he could take care of himself. It was getting late, we needed to be out there, why was he taking so much time? I couldn't wait anymore; I left the building walking down the street with a hood over my head so no one could recognize me. As I walked not knowing where I was going to, I saw the Ford Bronco yet again but this time, it wasn't the two of them, it was just one. I brought out my handgun, checked the cartridge to see if it was loaded, of course I knew it was loaded but it was just a safety measure. They weren't in their full strength, I could engage the ones I meet here, who knows, I could capture one of them who'd lead us to Daria. I snuck into the bar, had my berretta gun tucked in my trousers, I wasn't interested in causing a scene if I could get one with the least amount of gunshots.

I walk into the bar, I was stunned, and it was Daria. What was a lady like her doing in a place like this? That is so unlike her. Something wasn't right. She must have gotten wind that we were close by, or they've already gotten Harold, I was about to take my exit. It would be too risky to engage her now, the circumstance clearly wasn't favourable, and something was definitely off. I turned back quietly to exit the bar when I hear the words, her voice piercing through me like an arrow hitting its target, at once, one of the goons had blocked my exit. "Wouldn't you like to stay and have a drink? Your partner could really do with one right now". "I knew it, they had gotten Harold, but how? Did the agent he trusted so much sell him out? What in the actual bunkers was going on here?" It was like a viscous cycle, our mission. We'd look like we were in control one minute and the next we are in trouble. How did he get himself captured I couldn't tell but the odds were heavily stacked against us, I needed to think of something and fast if we were going to make it out of here alive?

"I don't remember him being a big fan of drinking "I said as I tried to turn back towards her direction, she had Harold sitting in the same table as her, he wasn't bound but had her gun in his face. My hands were just besides me, close to my berretta, I knew there'd be an opening and I could make a move, I had to be smart about it or he'd definitely get killed or I could even get killed myself. I had to keep up the conversation so she'd not just shoot us immediately, "Harold, how'd you end up like this?", he shook his head and looked at me, I could tell something huge had happened, he had probably been betrayed by his agent friend, "I told you to trust no one didn't I?" He continued talking "I wasn't wrong mate, in this world, there's only one person you can trust and that's yourself lad". My fears had caught up with me, he had been sold to the enemy.

"I have you both in one place finally, I can just kill the both of you and end this child's play. You didn't think you could escape, did you? I just wish you'd understand that this is bigger than you both, than all of us. This is an expansion to new horizons. You are all just too afraid to accept change. Humans fear what they don't understand". Daria snarled at us, I wasn't having any of it "you call this change, killing the weak? This is not the 11th century where you just wake up and take over, people have choices you know, they can choose not to be under you, it's allowed. I don't know where you get these ideas but what about change makes you think killing the British prime minister is right?" I cut in trying to give Harold a chance to give a signal or do something. Daria wanted us to know just how weak and insignificant we are to the whole plot, she was willing to remind us that even if we made it out of Russia, killed her, we'd never make it home alive "its survival of the fittest mate, the weak must give way for the strong, it's the natural order. As regards the prime minister, the decision to kill him came from within the English cabinet, it wasn't a Russian idea so I'd rather you fix your house before pointing fingers at others. Once I had rid the world of you both, I will send a message to England that you have both been killed and with no information forthcoming, your prime minister would be oblivious to his death. It's a script written in the fortunes of today. His death would mark a new beginning for both our nations. We'll build a super government and then we'll go after the entire world".

She believed in what she was saying, I could see the lust for power in her eyes. "You think others would fold their arms and watch you take over "I asked still waiting for a sign but a voice from behind me echoed throughout the room reminding us that we weren't attending a Q and A "let's just kill them Daria, they are stalling", it was the guy that had blocked my path. "Stalling you say? Who might you reckon we are waiting for? Our own nation sent us out here to die and it seems like die we shall", Harold cut in responding to him, he continued "at least let us know why we are dying, we deserve to know for what reason the United Kingdom is sacrificing us?" "Pitiful, pitiful. The UK government has nothing do with this. As far as most of your top intelligence officers are aware, I am supposed to help David bring you back home safe, Harold. I have someone else I work for, a key player in world politics, the weakness of your prime minister irritates him. You see an opportunity; you have to grab it by the scruff of its balls and not just sit idly by. I am not a big fan of killing the prime minister but look at the bigger picture here lads. You have been a bone in my throat, I must say but I would have been disappointed if two English agents were any less troublesome".

It was a gamble, but I had to take it anyways "who do you work for Daria Iyanov?" She smiled "what good would it do you to know?" She asked mockingly because she was ready to shoot at me. I continued "none, I'll die here and that information with me, but I wanted to know the scumbag that is on the verge of committing treason at its highest on his own country". She laughed, "I work for MI6 and I'm answerable to the prime minister as you are. The person I work for need not be mentioned but I will tell you something however, in 10 days, the prime minister will give his speech on the defence against the unknown in an indirect hit at the Russians, which would be the very last time, he'd speak to England or to anyone for that matter. I won't stain my arms with blood from the likes of you, shoot him Yuri".

This was it, right here in front of me, a huge Russian with a gun right in front of me, I was going to meet my maker, I clearly wasn't ready to go, I couldn't leave England in the hands of treacherous people, and I hadn't seen my wife since I found out she was pregnant. I closed my eyes waiting for my own death when I heard a gunshot, my feet trembled, the hairs on my skin stood upright. I held on to my stomach, applying pressure so I'd at least have a few seconds to live before passing to the great beyond. I fell on my feet and eventually on the floor. My time had come. This was it for me and maybe for the prime minister and everybody I knew and loved.

CHAPTER TWENTY-SEVEN: ONBOARD

The gun shot triggered a series of events that I never predicted, as I fell on the floor, I could hear Harold shouting, I was on the floor when I realized I was neither in pain nor was I bleeding. I hadn't been shot; it was Yuri that had been shot but who did the shooting. I got up, Harold had taken cover over the bar and Yuri was falling right beside me. It felt like time had stopped and those events were happening slowly when actually they were happening in normal time. I got up, ran towards Harold and I saw him docked with someone else besides him "who is this guy?" I asked unsure of what was going on, Harold replies "the guy who just saved your life David, this is Wayne, Wayne James. He's the agent I told you about that was undercover on project x". It made sense now, they planned the whole thing "hey, why wasn't I informed about the plan?" "Sorry lad, the lesser the better". I didn't care if I was informed or not, I was alive and that was the most important thing.

We all hid behind the bar counter, Wayne had a revolver, he wasn't going to stay armed for a while, the other guys had arrived, it was a three versus four shooting this time, it seemed a little fair but they had Akm rifles and we had a revolver and a berretta maximum 20 rounds between the both of us, it wasn't a shootout we could win. We had to get out of here. "What was the essence of this plan mate? Yeah, we shot one of them but is that why you staged this whole thing, just to kill one guy?" I yelled at him. "No, you arse, I needed her to say a few things, and I knew you'd push for it, your unending nationalism would push you to ask for answers even in the face of death. I banked on that, and it worked. Wayne's has with him an R2D2 recorder, he has all she said on tape, I know we don't have evidence yet, but she said a few things that we could work with".

Finding out we had some leverage was the best news I had heard since I came to Russia, we had to get the hell out of here, but I couldn't leave without Daria coming with us or at least dead. I held my berretta gently; it was now or never baby. I had a few cartridges with me so I could endure a prolonged shootout. The gun fire continued, "we need to get out of here" Wayne screamed, "there's a door out back, we just need to find our way out of here quickly". I looked at Harold, I was happy to see his filthy arse, we are close to making it out of here, we could go home together and see our families, I reached for my lower legs and brought out a 25 ACP baby browning placket pistol "oh I forgot, you can have this, we are going to need all the fire power we can get". He collected it, really pleased with my contributions to the plan. "I am going to cover you both, go through the back door and then you cover me" I suggested, and they agreed "alright, on my count, one, two, go" I got up. Shooting all over the place as fast as I can, the bullets not hitting anybody but breaking bottles and glasses just across the bar. The sounds of gunshots filled the air like there was a battle being fought in the bar.

Wayne and Harold were out, I needed a little cover to slip out, but the Akm rifle was stronger than the Acp, the revolver and the berretta that we had. It was going to be hard topping them. I was slowly running out of ammo and just about that time, like a miracle, we heard police sirens. It was strange but felt good to hear, I've been in Russia a while and had been involved in multiple shootouts, but this was the first time the coppers showed up, Daria and her goons stopped shooting responding to the sirens and I took advantage of that break. I ran outside as met up with Harold and Wayne who were already outside. We had to get out of there as fast as possible but Daria this time wasn't ready to let us go. The gunfire continued, it seemed Daria and her guys were exchanging with the coppers. It was good, for the first time, Russia was doing something good for me.

We needed to use that as a distraction for us to escape, we needed a vehicle, but none was anywhere close, the coppers were parked out front where Daria's Pontiac and her teams Bronco were parked and we couldn't get there. We had to escape on foot. We were running away, the gunshots still banging, the bystanders taking cover, it was a dark day, the covers of night stretched beyond her usual reaches, there was no moon in the sky, the cold Russian breeze gave the idea that it'd rain. It was already dropping blood in Tver like it had been for a while, the town could do with a little rain to wash away the deaths. We could do with a little rain to aid our escape. The path was broad, open, with no Alleys or hideouts or what not, we just had to run outside the periphery of their vision and that wasn't going to be easy.

Daria snuck out of the gun battle, she had two guys with her, the guys that were left kept the coppers busy, but she had with her goons that'd aid her in gunning us down and she didn't let herself down. As we ran, we heard a single gunshot, I ducked my head in a bid to avoid being shot, it looked like it had missed but that wasn't the case, Wayne was down, I wanted to stop and take him with me anyways, but he screamed at me "keep going lad, you have to get the fuck out of here". I wanted to stop but Harold warned against it, we got closer to the walls where the edges of the building would protect us from the bullets. We ducked as she started to walk over to us. The R2D2 recorded was still with Wayne, we had to get it off him before making our way. He laid there in the centre of the road with blood gushing out of his mouth, he could barely move, I cannot say exactly how death feels but I could see the sadness in his eyes knowing this was it.

Daria didn't know he had a recorder with him but she knew she had us cornered and we weren't running away. We were both ducked on different sides of the road, I was almost out of ammo, and Harold was out himself. He rushed in, I didn't know that that was the plan, when I saw him running out, I started to shoot as much as I can, Daria and the guys took cover on the walls of the building, and he picked up the recorder from Wayne's dead body and tossed it to me. I was out of ammo, I caught the recorder but just when he was about to run out of the road, I heard a single gunshot, I saw with my own two eyes, Harold's body moved back a little, his feet didn't move from the spot however. Blood dropped on the floor, drop after drop, I saw him as he fell on his knees, he looked at me, "run" he said. That was the last words I heard before a barrage of gunfire followed. Harold was taking multiple hits over his thorax. His body vibrated as each bullet pumped into his chest and stomach. He was never going to make it alive. He was living his life a day at a time before I met him, did I bring death on these innocent men?

This was no time to wallow, I got hold of the recorder and I looked at Daria, she and her men were running towards me, they weren't focused on shooting, this was my chance to make a run for it. I ran as fast as my legs could carry me, my heart beating even faster with every stride, I was weak and tired from my gunshot wound that hadn't healed completely but I couldn't afford to stop if I wanted to live. They chased after me, shooting every now and then hoping to hit me somehow. I ran, knowing I didn't have the chance to hide as they were right behind me, my chances of escape was slim, they wouldn't allow me a single word if they catch me this time, I ran, my breathing heavy as though my chest was congested, my pulse racing faster than I was. My feet stumping the ground as I made huge strides to avoid being caught. The sound of the gunshots from the bar had simmered down, someone had won the gun battle but who? The sound of sirens cried through the quiet night and I knew in my heart that the coppers had prevailed. I could run to them for safety but I remembered, the only lesson Harold taught me was trust no one, they'd hand me back to British authorities and whoever wanted me dead would have their way.

Daria was desperate, she chased after me, ignoring the blaring sirens just behind her, I was afraid as well but I banked on her desperation to get the better of her. It was in the dead of night and the constant gunshots had everyone in their houses, it was just me, Daria, her goons and the coppers that troubled the peace of the entire district. I needed to get off the road, I had to head for the houses, that way I could take cover from the bullets, I was out of ammo and couldn't exchange. I was too focus on Daria that I lost focus on myself. My legs caught an edge trying to make a hard left to avoid being caught, Thrown off balance, I fell on the floor, bracing my shoulder against the wall surface, pain shot through my arm, I couldn't scream not to attract attention, I yelled within my breath, the air left my lungs as I struggled to get back my breath. I had to keep going but without my arms, I could barely go far or even fast. I knew I had to take cover, I had just one cartridge left, this wasn't the right time to shoot at them or I could and attract the coppers attention, but I could be dead before they get here.

I pulled my broken body as I found my way into the open door of a building, I wasn't bleeding so they had no way to trace me, there were a couple of doors and they stopped trying to figure out where I had run to. The coppers sirens were losing grounds, it didn't scream as much as it could, maybe they had missed us, I was all on my own alone, I didn't go too far into the building, I had no reason involving more innocent people, none should die on account of me anymore. They were lots of building doors and I could have entered any one of them, they screened the environment thoroughly to be sure I had entered any one of the building. It was obvious I had entered one of them, they decided to split up to cover more grounds and save time. One of the goons, entered the building I was in and Daria and the other entered separate buildings.

I had them where I wanted them, I had split them up, I had plotted a divide and conquer strategy and it was working exactly the way I intended. I was injured and stood a greater chance if I took them one after the other. I had so much resentment in my heart for Daria and I knew I had less than 10 days if I was going to save the prime minister. I hid still underneath the stairs in the building as I watched him walk past me with his gun stationed in front of his body. I had to disarm him to even the playing field, I knew I couldn't cause too much damage or any damage to him if I couldn't get him to drop his gun.

I jumped him, throwing his gun on the ground, it was man for man, pound for pound although he outsized me, it was as even as it could get, the fighting scene. He said with a heavily accented voice "tonight, you die punk", I wasn't ready to die yet, I curled my fist and aimed for his lower jaw, he blocked with his left hand, landing a hard blow down my lower abdomen, pain shot through my gut running straight for my brain, I felt his fist against my bowels. He clearly had more experience than me, I could have shot him I thought but that would attract the others. Taking this one down would be too much work, two would be impossible. He laughed at me as I fell on my knees to the floor, blood splattered all over the floor from my mouth. It wasn't like I thought it would be in my head. I pulled myself up, clenched my fist, harder this time, we go again. I went for a low blow this time, hitting his lower abdomen but unlike his earlier punch, mine didn't do much damage, he returned the Favour punching me right on my jaw, the pressure was strong sending me tumbling down the hard floor.

I thought the playing field was even but it clearly wasn't, he had the upper hand in this fight and if it continued, I'd be dead. I knew I had to act smart and fast. I wasn't going to give up, not now, Harold,

Wayne. Their names rested on my lips as I clenched both fists this time." striking a pose with my right leg slightly forward and the left behind. He approached me fiercely, swinging his right fist at me, I evaded it, holding his head, I banged it against the rails of the stairs, blood splattered all over, he was clearly in disarray at that moment, I attacked him punch after punch, right hand, left hand after each other, I couldn't afford him space to cover himself or attack me back. I kept throwing punch after punch and when he was barely standing, I banged his head against the wall sending the huge man tumbling down the floor. He was out cold. I had won yet another battle but the war waged on.

Battered and bruised, I tried to make my escape, I headed for the door but Daria and the last goon were there, I could hear them talk "where's Zhirkov?", she asked "he went into that building", the man responded, she continued "why isn't he out? Something must have happened to him. Go check it out", he walked in carefully, not wanting to be caught off guard. I had the element of surprise and I also had a berretta in my hand, I wasn't ready to get into another fist fight with anyone, I was going to lose the next one even if my opponent was a child. If I shoot at him as well, Daria would hear and return fire. I watched him from a floor above as he climbed carefully up the stairs, I left his partner right there on the floor, I needed the distraction. He climbed the stairs quietly, his boots made no sound, his breath louder than the sound of his feet. He was still, gently he walked hoping to catch me off guard but he was sore mistaken. I've had him in my sights the enter time. He came up on the open floor and found his partner lying lifeless on the floor, he approached to check for pulse and I jumped him, holding firmly to my berretta, I struck the back of his head with the magazine sending him tumbling to the ground. He was out cold as well.

The odds were in my Favour, I was going to celebrate but my joy was short lived, Daria was just behind me. She shot at me but missed, I ran through the passageway heading for a small window at the end, the individual doors of each houses were locked and the only possible escape route was through the window at the end of the passageway. I jumped through the window landing on that same shoulder that I had sprained earlier. The pain shot up finding its way to my brain. I screamed in agony as she took more shots at me, aiming to kill me as I struggled to run. She was desperate and pursued after me without her goons. She wanted so bad to tie loose ends that she had made when she delayed in killing me.

I ran through the street, she followed after me, she had lost her patience, she shot like a madman all over the place and after a while, she stopped, it seems she was out of ammo, all I could hear was the click of the rifle as she pressed against the trigger. She was out, this was my chance, I wasn't going to hesitate, she was out in the open. Her desperation had got the better of her. I got up from my hiding spot with my berretta held firmly in my right hand, I looked at her straight into her eyes, it was like I could see her soul, she wailed on the inside, her life had been full of mistakes but on the outside, she looked like she had it all under control. I wasn't going to make the same mistake she made, I wasn't interested in her chit chat, I knew all I needed to and I would act on that knowledge. I held firmly my berretta, she was going to say something just before I pulled the trigger, the lead soaring through the air, meeting her right between her eyes, her blood splattered, filling the space in front of her face as her dead body fell to the ground, I was satisfied, I had avenged Wayne and Harold. Now, what I needed to do was fix the bug within the higher ups of the United Kingdom. I didn't know who was responsible yet but if I could save the prime minister, I could find out.

CHAPTER TWENTY EIGHT: HOME SWEET ENGLAND

I buried Harold and Wayne not far from the abandoned building, it was sad as I couldn't bring them home, maybe I could do something about that when this was over. Harold had a picture of his wife and kids that he always carried around, I took it with me, I knew I needed to pay a visit to his wife and his boys whenever I got back to England.

I had to plan my exit, I still couldn't contact HQ, I didn't know who would be on the other end of the phone. I needed to sneak back into England. I had a little over nine days to save the prime minister and clear out the system. He had put so much trust in me, I had to repay the favour.

I couldn't fly into England, I was sure the Russia government and a fair part of the English government would be looking for me, I had to go in quietly. The docks was the best option, I could sneak in one of the vessels headed for London and in a couple of days I'd be home and dry. It was a perfect plan, Tver was a port city, it'd be easier to find a vessel headed my way here than any other place in Russia.

Time wasn't my friend. It was morning already. That was the longest night of my life. The coppers, I never knew what happened to them, they never came back. So many things didn't make sense to me but I didn't have the time to figure them out. I left the grave site heartbroken for my friends but eager for the adventure that waited for me in England.

The whole incident happened not far from the Saratov port at Tver. It was a small port just off the town. I was lucky enough to get there just before the MS korotkov left, it was bound for the dame's port in London. How fortunate I was, it was a 2338 kilometres sailing from Tver to Dames port which was in Kent. Once in Kent, I'll board a train to London. I needed to keep a low profile. I needed to think fast and act smart if I was going to save his life. This was my biggest test yet, watching the prime minister die in public would cause major upset in London, it'd mark the beginning of a breakdown. I couldn't have that happening to the country I loved so much.

There were guards at the entrance of the Korotkov but that wouldn't stop me, it was a vessel transporting construction materials from Russia to England. On board was Russian security personnel and a few boat workers. At this point in my life, I had seen too much to trust any Russian. I avoided the security and hid in one of the cargo that was on board the vessel, I snuck out just before another cargo was placed on top.

I found my way to the chain locker. That would be my hiding spot for the rest of the trip. I overheard from the captain that it was a 7day trip to England. That wasn't the best news as I had just nine days to stop the assassination of the prime minister. I had to go back to England as quickly as possible.

I was nowhere close to being comfortable, I wasn't much of a sea person so I stayed inside the chain locker room as much as I can. I had no business being outside, I didn't want confrontations with the crew. I was so happy on the inside. Regardless of what happens now, even if I die, I'd die on English soil, unlike Harold and Wayne, I'd be buried at home. I was heading to England, but I knew it wasn't going to be smooth sailing from here. Like the Korotkov, I still had wave like obstacles to overcome but I had come too far to give up now.

Everything I had been through since I joined the service had prepared me for this. This was the moment for which I was born. The trip was hitch free except for those times when the vessel would battle waves bigger than her, she'd swerve from right go left, tilting so slant I sometimes thought she'd fall into the sea. The waves never stopped the vessel. She faced her adversity and every time she did, through sheer persistence, she'd overcome them.

Seven days, locked in a small room was driving me mad, I counted days as I prayed for the vessel to get to London. I was already losing myself being in there without seeing sunlight. I hadn't had a decent meal in forever. I survived on snacks that I smuggled with me on board the Korotkov. It was not a good way to live but who was I to complain? Harold lived in a building that could kill him at any time but he managed to make friends just to stay off grid. His was the biggest service to country I had ever seen. I needed to emulate his resolve, his love for England was real, without blemish. His life was the true case of an agent living and dying for his country. He was worthy of a medal of honour for bravado and commitment. I had been honoured by the prime minister for my service to my country but I was a nobody compared to people like Harold and Wayne

I was in my self-inflicted solitary confinement when the anchor started to drop, we were stopping. That means one thing, we are at dame's port. We were in Kent, we were in England. All I had to do was take a train to London but I couldn't even tell if it was day or night. I needed to be in London at night and I needed a plan of action. Running into the prime minister's residence would make it impossible to find out whoever was behind this, I needed the assassin to act, he alone could tell me who he worked for. I snuck out of the chain locker, the sun was setting. I felt the English air blow through my hair, I heard people speak in English language that I could understand without straining my ears too much. Yes this was England, this was home but what date was it?

I left the Korotkov in a hurry, got to the train station that wasn't very far from the dame's port, it helped transport products to where they were needed across England. There was a shipment headed for London. It was just an hour train ride from Kent to London and I boarded.

Conflicted on where to go to once I was in London, I thought about not telling the prime minister of my plans, I was going to use him as bait, I couldn't contact Carla, she'd freak out, I couldn't tell my parents or hers as well. I wasn't a friend person and didn't have friends outside of work. All the friends I had made were in the line of duty and they had all died serving their country. I had to somehow navigate around London without being found out, enough to save the prime minister's life and save the country. The train ride from Kent to London unlike the sail was calm, the breeze blew rippled through my body as I admired the English country side, I never wanted to leave home but I knew it was only a matter of time before it'd happen again. I looked a mess, my beards were sticking out and my skin broken and bristled for lack of care. I could do with a lot of care but that was secondary.

In no distant time, I was in London, I rushed over to my house, even if I couldn't go in, it'd do me a world of good to just look at Carla from afar off but to my greatest surprise, I got there and the house was deserted, it looked like Carla had not been home since I left, I wouldn't blame her. I approached the door unsure of how I'd feel if I went in. The key was right where I left it, I was a little heartbroken that she left and never came back to see if I had return.

I couldn't stay mad at Carla, I left her when she needed me the most, it was my fault. I needed to get back to her and be a part of her life. I opened the door and went in, it was the first night in a couple of days that I had slept well.

Entering the house, the first thing I needed to check was a calendar, I couldn't account for how long I was at sea. I was in a room where I neither saw the sun nor the moon. I had lost track of time being in the chain lockers. It was the 13th of October 1983, the prime ministers speech was the next day, it had been planned for months, it was scheduled for the 14th of October 1983, I barely just made it in time. I couldn't stop now, I had to finish what I started.

I took a warm bath, shaved my beards and slept in the bed I share with my darling wife, it was a lonely night, but it was better than the sleepless nights I had in Russia, I could barely sleep. Even if I wanted to, I had to inform the prime minister of what was going on and my plan of action, I needed him to play along to help me apprehend the culprit. I had to solve the problem on my own. I was on the couch and turned on the TV, the news on BBC one only had one thing to say, and it was the prime minister's speech by midday tomorrow, it wasn't doing me any good constantly hearing about it all over TV.

It was a briefing to all of England and it was going to happen just outside the House of Lords. It was an outside event, I thought. It couldn't be any other means of execution but sniping. I had to find out the best possible spot and wait for the assassin to show up.

The night wouldn't move. It had all come to this. The silence of the night brought calm over my aching body, the calmness was the cure I needed after hearing gunshots throughout my time in Russia. I wasn't where I wanted to be yet but it felt good knowing I was no longer behind enemy lines. I had left hostile territory, I was home. Home sweet England. I could barely sleep and I knew why.

I had so much pressure building up within me, my friend and prime minister of England could be killed today and it'd be because I made the singular choice of not stopping the speech today but if prevented him from being killed today without apprehending the person behind it, they'd easily just try tomorrow and the day after that and the day after that until they'd get him eventually. I had to end it once and for all. I was too anxious to wait for the sun to come up. I heard the birds sing their songs, their sweet tunes of newness, it was a chance to try harder anytime I heard the birds sing. I had been privileged to be alive, a lot of others couldn't boast the same privilege, Harold, Wayne, they'd wish to be alive but they weren't. I had to fulfil the mission Harold started, I'd like to fight the cause Wayne believed in, he could have betrayed us and he'd still be alive this very moment but he chose to stand, fight and die for his country.

I wore a jacket and a baseball cap, the plan was to remain unseen by any who'd recognize me, the prime minister was going to have a meeting with the parliament in the House of Lords just before the big speech just outside the building. I had to infiltrate his security detail without being noticed. Being seen would change the tides of events. I couldn't call him, I knew the number of desks his call go through before they get to him. I didn't know who to trust anymore. Everybody was guilty until proven innocent to me at the time.

I headed for Downing Street contemplating my next course of action. The day was wide awake with people going about their everyday lives, cars moving through the streets, the sounds of their horns going off. This was London, a town that speak even for itself. I got close and noticed his convoy was there, armoured vehicles with tinted glasses, it wasn't unattended, but the security guards had their focus on ensuring he got in safely. They had their guards down not expecting anything, but I knew at that point that his life was constantly in danger until I got whoever wanted him dead.

I had to get in those vehicles somehow else I couldn't save him, I was as close as can be, but I didn't know how to go beyond the current spot I was in. I knew I was supposed to save his life when an ambulance rushing on call blasted her siren as she drove speedily just besides the convoy, the guards immediately formed a protective shield around the prime minister. It was a Miracle of some sort but with the attention of everyone around on the vehicle, I snuck in. I knew the particular one he uses, I was in charge of his security detail after all. I was in, I stayed calm on the floor, nobody had noticed, I guessed but that had luck written over it.

I stayed still and after the ambulance had gone it's way, the door of the car was opened and he walked in, sat down, it was pitch black in the car and I got up and said as quietly as I could "Good morning sir", he was shocked almost out of his skin, he wanted to run away or scream but I calmed him down " calm down sir, it's me David, David Scarlet", he was calm the moment he heard my name, I could see the joy in his expression as he hugged me close, he wasn't willing to let go but I freed myself, I had something important I needed to talk to him but he was too eager to talk "David old' boy, what in the devil are you doing here? Aren't you supposed to be in Russia or something?" He was oblivious to what was going on but I had the chance to inform him, "Sir, I have a lot to tell you, you just have to listen and do exactly as I say". He was puzzled, I wasn't smiling as I used to, I had an expression that said all wasn't fine. He knew he had to listen to me and now "what is going on lad", I had so much to say but no time to say it all. I had to start from somewhere however "Sir, I know you know about the takeover plot in Russia, it's bigger than that sir, they are building weapons, chemical weapons they are planning on creating a super government made up of a few European nations to eventually take over more than just Europe".

He wasn't exactly surprised "I'm well aware mate, I turned it down, the proposal was tempting but it'd send the world back into war, we can't relive the world wars again, the world might not survive it this time". That response made me believe that they were people I could still trust and he was one of them, I continued "I know you'd never do that sir but that's where the problem arises, there are people within the cabinet that would and the Russians already have teamed up with them. The major agenda is taking your life". With you out of the way, they'd have someone who would key to it, the person might not necessarily be a bad person but he'd key into the very idea of a European dominance over the world. It's supposed to happen today, your death that is". He was shocked, he was working into a land mine the whole time but he wasn't aware. "What do you recon we do son?" He asked unsure if he should cancel the speech. "I have it under control sir, but I'm going to need your help", "anything lad, anything you want, I am giving you the go ahead completely" he said.

I get closer to him as I told him the plan just to be sure nobody else knew, the driver couldn't see or hear much as there was a dark tempered glass between us and him but I wasn't taken any chances, I got close and I reduced my voice "you are going to get shot like they intended", he wasn't having any of that "what in Fucks name are you talking about mate? I am not Superman or something, if I get shot, I will die". "I know that sir but you will wear a vest, I need to know where the shots coming from, if I can't find the perfect shooting spot before the speech, I need to use you to locate the shooter. I know it's not going to be easy, but I can't just have you stop the speech. It'd just delay them for today but they'd keep trying and who knows when they'll succeed. We must end this once and for all".

He liked the plan, we were still talking when the car stopped, I had to go out somehow but I couldn't be seen, he ordered the car be driven to the parking lot, he wanted to see some parts of the building that he hadn't seen in a while, after all he had arrived early. The driver obliged and the car was driven to the back, he came down, left the door open for me as he walked round the lot. I snuck out unseen and went about to sort more answers.

CHAPTER TWENTY NINE: UNMASKED

The session with parliament had begun, English men and women filled the street with Britain's flags in their hands. It was a big day for all of England. Deliberations were on going to confirms Britain's stance against Russia's push for power, the outcome will define the relationship between Russia and England over the years to come. Journalists from all media houses across the world stood anxiously waiting for the prime minister's speech, it was a busy place and a busy day, I had noticed the tallest point a few hundred meters away from the venue of the ministerial speech. It seemed the perfect spot for a sniper.

The prime minister was on a vest but what if he got hit on the head, I hadn't thought of a plan for that. I needed some guarantee that he'd shoot from that point. I had to take a gamble, a huge gamble.

I left where I was, headed for the point when the prime minister came out from the session, it was beginning, the speech, I had to get there real fast, I ran up the stairs, my heart throbbing, my breath coming as fast as it could, I couldn't leave anything to chance, I got to the top but it was empty. Nobody there, just me, I stood there confused, not knowing what next I had to do. I had miscalculated something, somewhere, I was in more of a situation than I had ever been, I needed to get back to the prime minister, I could be a human shield and take the bullet but except the shooter delayed, I was never going to get there in time, I turned running fast towards the stairs when I heard the sound of a gun, I turned back, ran to the edge to see what would happen next, the prime minister took the shot to the chest. I had seen the shooter. He was in a building just a few meters away from the one I was on.

I would never meet up if I ran down the stairs and up the stairs of the building, it was a jump I could make, he had left his spot, apparently, he saw me and hurriedly took the shot, I ran as fast as my legs could carry me, I stepped over the edge, I threw myself up so high in the air, moving my legs from the back and then forward to propel me forward, I made the Jump landing on my feet, he had gone through the stairs, he could be anywhere I thought but just as I was about to go through the door of the stairs, he came out running, not accounting that I was there and as hard as I could, I clenched my fist, making my knuckles as hard as I could and threw it at him, he was in motion and my knuckles also in motion, making the contact crisp and fierce. It sent him tumbling down the ground. He was out cold but why did he run back up, I wanted to confirm, it was then I saw the prime minister's personal guards running up there. I knelt with my hands behind my head not willing to cause any problems.

They got to where I was, saw him lying lifeless. Some of the guards wanted to apprehend me on the charge that I was a culprit of the crime but one of the guards advised against it "that's the prime minister's personal guard", he said as he gestured towards me. Those words sent a shiver down my spine. For the majority of two months, I was a fugitive running around Russia with assassins on my trail, I had smuggled my way out of Russia back to London but in an instant, I was restored to where I ought to be. It was over. Tears rolled down my cheeks as I stood up. I looked over the edge, the prime minister had been taken away. The guards demanded the criminal but I refused, I am going to bring him in, don't you worry about that, after minutes of arguing who gets to turn him, the same guard who identified me agreed that I be allowed to do that.

I held him firmly like a football captain his trophy so not a single scratch would come on it, I wasn't going to take any chance. I demanded a vehicle by the time I was down, and drove off with the culprit.

I got to the safe house as instructed by the prime minister and proudly I dragged him through the hallway and by the time I was at the interrogation room, the prime minister was there waiting for me. "You didn't protect me you know, I got shot and that fucking hurts like hell, you know?" He laughed, I could barely laugh myself, I needed to uncover who was behind this plot once and for all and I needed a long vacation off duty after this. "You are too stubborn to die anyway ", I responded as I smiled pushing him on the chair to give him a little comfort before I break every bone in his body for answers. I didn't have the x serum but I could make him talk the old fashion way.

He was firm, resolute, refusing to spill hoping we'd torture him till death came. I wasn't going to leave his sight for a second because I knew people were waiting for me too. The prime minister surprisingly didn't leave either. He was as curious as I was to know who wanted to kill him and take England to war. It had been going on for hours, he was bleeding from every opening in his face and even parts of his body that didn't open gushed blood. He was resolute, I'd do with an X serum right about now but there was no where I could get it from. I could still go on, I went on and on, torture technique after torture technique. I wasn't going to kill him, I just wanted him to go beyond his endurance threshold and he'll spill.

I had nowhere to be except right there. The prime minister had been proclaimed dead to the public, England was in panic, the arrest of the culprit had been left under the rug, and nobody knew he was ever caught. Whatever happened here was between a few individuals, it was classified. The interrogation went on for hours and eventually he spilled. He named names and sent shock down our spines. The prime minister visibly disgusted that someone he calls a friend was behind his planned death. With blood all over his face, he agreed to speak "I'll talk, no more, no more please". I was interested and I asked, "go on with it mate, that way, you won't die here", he could barely talk but I heard the word Jim leave his mouth. I didn't know a Jim, but the reaction of the prime minister clearly suggested knew one, he was sad, angry. He walked away from the desk; he was visibly heartbroken. "Who is Jim Sir?" I asked curiously wanting to know. "Jim Potter" he said barely willing to say the words. Now the name makes sense, it was the secretary of defence, Jim Potter. "What the fuck is this world turning into? He oversees security in the fucking country, how could he sell us out so easily?"

That was it, I had seen it through, and I sighed with relief, as I left the room. The prime minister followed me, appreciating me for the work done, I looked at him, clenched my fist, he could tell there was so much emotion running through me. "I wasn't done hone here sir, I had to make this arrest, I had to look him in the eye as I took him to jail. For Harold's sake and for Wayne's sake and for every other agent that dies out there in defence of their country, I had to lock up this bastard". The prime minister knew I had seen so much in Russia that I wasn't thinking of anything but putting this man out for good. He nodded his head, pat me on the shoulders and said to himself "go do what you have to son".

We left the safe house at about 3:00 pm in the afternoon, the house was located on the outskirts of town. As we drove back to the heart of London, the scenery brought me to tears and to the realization that all this was soon to be over. I could go back home and be with Carla but first I had to pay a visit to Harold's wife and his two boys, I had to give them the picture and let them just how much respect I have for their husband and father and tell them just how proud England should be of him. The tears rolled down my cheeks completely visible to the prime minister who sat just a few inches away from me, but he never asked what the problem was. He allowed me to detoxify my thoughts, he just sat there smiling the whole time.

We arrived back at London, made our way to Buckingham were members of parliament had conveyed in the name of bringing calm to London. I saw in one place, more journalists than I had seen my enter life. The streets of London buzzed. The assassination of the prime minister was huge. It was another Kennedy incident and people wanted clarity. It was quite the scene when the car stopped just in front and the prime minister came down, the journalists and everyone at the scene paused for a minute trying to understand what was going on, they saw him take a bullet to the chest and watched him go down, hence it was difficult to understand what they were seeing. Once the realization had hit them that the prime minister made it through, the silence turned instantaneously to an incredible roar of joy. It could be heard as far as Russia. I smiled as I walked in on the right side of the prime minister. I could only imagine the expression on the face of the secretary of defence.

The next few minutes was dramatic, he thought about apologizing as I placed the cuff on him, then he tried to run but I was determined more than anything. He was taken away for interrogations, he gave up some names, and a few high-profile government personnel were involved. Like Harold had wanted, I was cleaning the British government and Agency. My job here was done but I still had a thing or two I needed to do. The prime minister called me and asked, "how can I thank you for what you've done?" Tears rolled down my cheeks again as he asked. I gave him the address of where I buried Harold and Wayne. "Those are the true heroes' sir, please bring their bodies back home anyway you can. Place them close to their family sir. That's all I ask for now". I was about to walk away when I turned back, I had another request "oh sir, I could use a little time off and it should not be mentioned that I had returned to the agency". "Take as much as you want. Your country thanks you for your selfless service, lad". I walked away without saying anymore words. It was finally time to return home.

CHAPTER THIRTY: FALLEN APART

Whatever would happen next, I wasn't sure, arrests would be made but that wasn't for me to involve myself. My job was done, I had to go back home to settle issues with my wife since I had settled England's problems but first, I had to go to Harold's. His was in the suburbs just out of town. I had my baseball cap on, I took the drive in a cab from London to the address he had given me, it was a small home, he had a plan from when he returned, see out his days in the countryside with the love of his life and his kids but that was not to be. I knocked gently on the door and two kids; boys opened it before a lady walked right behind them. I could hardly hold back the tears as I saw the kids, she knew almost at once that something had happened to Harold. She started crying as well, her hands covered her mouth not to startle the kids, I hugged her, gave her the photo. I said to her "more men like Harold and England would be the greatest country on the planet. Your country thanks you for your sacrifice and for your husband's bravery". I saluted her and then I walked away.

It was time to fix my own home. I knew Carla went home so I left at once for my parents, it was already night fall, the darkness of night covered over the day like a blanket, the transition from the setting evening sun to the dark of night was gentle. The evening heat had given way for the gentle night breeze. Thoughts filled my head as I headed home but amidst all those thoughts, there was none of regret. I lost partners but they died in service to her majesty and England.

The major thought on my mind was how Carla would receive me. I was conflicted but she always knew how to handle my conflicts.

I got down from the cab, as I walked towards the door, I could hear my heart beat for uncertainty of what was to follow, I didn't knock on the door, I wanted to surprise them all, I opened the door, my father and mother were asleep on each other on the couch, it was my mom who saw me first as I walked in, she let out a loud cry that woke up my father who hugged me closely, my mom was still so emotional, she held on to me for longer than my dad but I freed myself.,

I had to see Carla I beckoned on them and the moment I said so, their countenance changed. "What is the problem?" I asked wanting to know why they had become sad suddenly. I knew they could tell me, but they didn't, my mom held me by the hand and walked into my old room, Carla was on my bed, covered up to her neck.

I didn't understand "is she sick? Why haven't you taken her to a hospital? What about the baby?" My mom started crying and it dawned on me, both their faces looked like they had been crying. I was confused, starting to get worried when I heard my name "David, is that you?" It was Carla, she was talking to me. I rushed over to her side, held her hand "it's me baby, I'm back now, I don't know what the problem is, but we'll manage it together ". She started crying as well. I didn't know what the problem was, but I couldn't only find out if someone told me. I walked over to my dad who was the only one besides me in the house that wasn't crying.

I needed to know what was going on, he held my hand as walked outside the room, he looked at me sad, "I didn't want you to meet us in this condition but despite how hard we tried to make it all look and feel good, we just couldn't", I clearly didn't understand what he was talking about and I clearly wasn't in the mood for time wasting. He noticed I lacked the patience to listen to what he was saying the way he was saying it, he continued "Carla, had a miscarriage, she lost your baby, she felt alone and needed you most at the time, but you weren't here to give her the comfort she needed". I was the problem the entire family was like this. I was out saving the country, the continent and preventing a war in the future and I couldn't save my own family.

My father wasn't done, he had more to say, and my show of impatience meant he kept throwing news at me that I wasn't ready to hear but had to anyways. He continued, "she was distraught, there was nothing your mom or I could say that would cheer her up, there was nothing her parents could say either that would cheer her up. She thought in her heart that she had failed you as a wife. According to her, it wasn't the first time she was losing a baby". That was the part of it all that broke me the most, right under my nose, my wife had been going through a lot, but I didn't know. I was so focused on the good times that I didn't notice she was going through a lot personally. He wasn't done, he had more to break my heart with after all, he was trying to be gentle, but I wouldn't have it. He continued, "just last week, she got up, told us that she needed to clear her head, that she needed a vacation of some sort. We didn't know what was going on with her and couldn't stop her from going, we only asked where she was going to but refused to spill telling us she would be fine and that she would be back in just over a week. We received the most shocking calls of our lives three days ago. She had flown to Greece where she attempted suicide, she took overdose of paracetamol in a bid to take her own life". He paused to allow me process what he had said. I could barely find the words to describe how I was feeling. I had been through so many near death experiences in my life, but none scared me like what my father just said.

Carla could barely move, I was out saving England, dodging bullets, engaging in high-speed chases, but the one person that needed more than anything, I couldn't be there for her. Carla had attempted suicide I thought to myself, I walked back into the room, saw her lying there unable to express the joy that I know she felt after seeing me. I couldn't process exactly what she was going through, but I wanted to be there for her. I was going to take time off and be there for my wife.

December 25, 2006

I laid on the bed, staring at the ceilings having my experiences flash through my mind's eyes. I had done a lot to save England, but I let my family sleep away from my hand, Carla had been through a lot with me and I can't help but think that if I was there for her, she wouldn't have gone through all the suffering she went to. We've been married a while and still we had no children. The statement my father made thirty-one years ago about Carla feeling like she had let me down haunted me till this day. I would have done like she did, taking my own life if she had lost hers either during the loss of the baby or the attempted suicide but that she is still alive is hope for us.

I turned to my side, Carla laid right next to me, there was however some inches of space between us, I closed the gap, held her firmly. I was in love with her like I was when I met her but why were we going through all these issues. It was easy for me to resolve to die for my country, but I wasn't giving as much to my marriage. I held Carla from behind and I felt as she snuggled up into me, it felt like old times.

I planted a gentle kiss on her neck, and she smiled gently but she didn't turn back. It wasn't over for us; I was going to make things work. What if we had no children, I was all the children she needed. I needed to let her know that she had not failed me. I was all she needed, and she was all I needed. I wanted to wake her up and tell her my resolve, but I hesitated not wanting to wake her up and ruin the moment but it seemed she was already up and she told me "If there is something you want to say to me, you best be saying it now" but this time she wasn't snarling, she was as gentle as she was the day I met her. I turned her over to me and told her as calmly as I could "I am going to make things right; we have a long way ahead of us and I wouldn't want to spend that time with any other person but you. Let's get help like you've always wanted". She smiled at me, she said nothing but nodded her head and snuggled even closely to me.

The night was slow, peaceful, and blissful. The gentleness of night spread all over the room, I could hear Carla's heartbeat against mine as she slept off. I could tell she was as happy as she wanted to be. Mark and Laura who were past their prime years still cared a lot for her and indeed the both of us. I noticed them enter the room twice trying to ascertain the conditions we were in. I saw them but I made no move to respond. I was trying to fall asleep as my mind travelled through my life, I subconsciously went back to 1986.

February 02, 1986

I had resumed at the GCHQ, locked out of access to information, to files and records, the accident was fresh, and I was having a mental and nervous breakdown. Nothing made sense, I had put away all the people in the service that had wanted me dead. The secretary of defence, Jim Potter had been locked up, a few top brass government officials had gone down with him, why then was I a target, I had to do something about it and fast before they strike again, who knows, this time they might succeed.

There was only one way to unravel this mystery and that would be to find the van and whoever was driving it, the night it ran me over. I had to go into full Sherlock Holmes mode. I paid attention to every detail, I observed everyone at HQ, whoever looked at me funny, I suspected them. I spent the next few days being on the lookout. The van was nowhere to be seen. It did look very familiar to me, I knew it was a reconnaissance vehicle, but who would be that careless? Who would try to take an agents life using an agency vehicle?

Weeks had gone by, work was unbearable, I could hardly focus, everything frightened me, I was almost driven mad with fear that they might strike again. A white van wasn't unusual in London, I didn't know where to start from, but I stumbled upon a boost in my investigation as I was on my own home, a white van with black windows with the last number 496, it was right there in front of me. I couldn't confront the people around it; it was a gang and I had no evidence to prove. My judgement would be branded irrelevant if my physical or mental health was deemed unfit. I needed a confession. I stopped driving over at a bar just across the road and watched them, a guy in denim in his mid-thirties entered the van and drove away. I followed him closely although not too close not to be too suspicious. He drove to a part of town that not just anyone lived. It was a high-profile part of town.

I wondered why a raggedy looking man was driving up an elite estate, I was shocked to my bones when I saw who he was meeting up with. Was she involved in all these? If she was, why wasn't she locked up like the rest of them? I spent the next few days tailing the white van. It seemed to me like the movement to take out the prime minister wasn't dead yet. It would only stop when he was dead, but I wasn't ready to let them succeed now, I followed him closely. I was more than ready to burst him whenever it felt right.

I needed an opening to get him down, but none was forthcoming. It was clear to me that she was desperate for revenge as the opening I sought after came looking for me. The guy in the white van came again to finish what he had started. I tailed him off a boy from

London, he was headed in the direction of my house, I didn't know why but he could have been headed anywhere, I didn't have to be paranoid, I followed him anyways and I wasn't wrong, he was headed for my house.

He had on him, a berretta 92 with a silencer placed on the nozzle. It was ironic that he tried to kill me with a gun that I loved so much. Carla was inside or so I thought, turns out that she found herself going over a lot to my parents as I had made a habit of staying out late night. I followed quickly as he headed for my room, if Carla was there, then she was in danger. The house was pitch black, Carla had a fear for everything and killed electricity when she goes out. I knew when I noticed the darkness that Carla was definitely not around, I could go all out on the intruder, but I needed no interference if I wanted to get a confession from him.

He went in, found his way to my room, I knew I didn't have to go in with him, I waited just underneath the stairs with a club in my hand. He had gone into the room dissatisfied that he hadn't seen anyone. Little did he know that it'd be the last he'd be out around town? He had just walked pass me when I came out from hiding, I said "hey" and when he turned round to find out who was behind him, I hit hard enough to knock him out but not enough to kill. I duck taped him and dragged him down to the basement.

I was going to do it again; I was going to do the whole tape recorder thing all over again. I hid my tape as I tied to him to a chair, he didn't need to know I was recording our conversation. He woke up at morning. I had called Carla and told her not to come home that morning, she asked why, and I had no real reason, but she didn't show up however. I had him in the basement with me, he spoke to me, and he clearly wasn't English, his accent was Russian, and I understood why he was involved in all this, I wasn't sure if he was an agent or not but I doubt he was because he couldn't tell I had been on him for a while. He was a henchman, but Rosa was stupid enough to deal directly with him, maybe because she thought the issue had died down and I wasn't fit to give a statement in court, but I was going to get evidence here and now.

He wasn't hard hearted like the sniper, he broke before the interrogation became intense, he confessed. He told me how he had been in London for a while, working closely for Rosa and Jim Potter. He continued to talk as I watched him blurt out all his rubbish. I allowed him talk as much he could. He said to me "you are only a small fish in a huge pond, you might kill me, but more would come after me, you can't stop us, we will get our wish". I laughed at his stupidity, and I told him "I can't stop the entire federation but one after another, I would stop you". I wasn't going to kill him.

I took the tape I had recorded over to the prime minister's office. He was at a meeting with some top officials, Rosa inclusive, I demanded to be let in but I was prevented, the security service men refused me entrance but I took the element of surprise, I was in. he was shocked to see me, angry might I add but he knew that there must have been a perfectly good reason why I would interrupt. "What is it lad?" he asked me, eager to know why I had forced my way into a Security Council meeting.

I looked at Rosa, shook my head, I brought out my recorder and the tape played, it had all the content that the Russian in my basement had mentioned. Rosa the whole time had been working with the Russians to topple his government and put in somebody that would give in to their inhumane call for war. The entire room was met with silence, Rosa cowered her head in shame, unable to defend herself as the prime minister gave the order for her to be carried away. I was still disabled as I twitched and randomly said words without being asked but I was satisfied with what I had done yet again for England.

I was honoured at the Security Council meeting for my bravado but deactivated shortly after for health purposes. The decision was shocking, but I understood, I needed to get better. I knew I'd be reactivated, when I wasn't sure, but I believed in the system. There would be ups and downs but what fun would the secret service be if every now and then, these kinds of actions don't avail themselves?

CHAPTER THIRTY-ONE: REACTIVATION

January 5, 2007

The festive periods were over, Carla and I had started seeking help, psychologists for her depression as well for my scars. That wasn't all, we were seeing a counsellor for our marriage. Things were looking up. I had been deactivated so long that I had grown used to my current job as private security for a corporation.

We had clearly moved on, I was feeling a little better, the seizures were still there every now and then, but the involuntary speeches had reduced drastically. We were doing very fine. The extended family were happy, and all was rosy. I took Carla out for breakfast on a certain evening, and it started all again, I was sent back to the life of a secret service agent. The bill that our waiter brought for us had 101 written underneath the cost. That was my call but what more adventure was I to expect in the service. I didn't know but I was going to answer the clarion call.

Death looms over me every minute of the day, twisting and turning, grinding my mind and body into turmoil, in to how, where and most importantly when I will end my life.

Printed in Great Britain
by Amazon

80612095R00119